# A Miracle for Mayfield

BY Gregory F. Wasylak

Llumina Press

ISBN: 978-1-62550-433-3

"Forgiveness is the answer to the child's dream of a miracle by which what is broken is made whole again..."
Dag Hammarskjold.

# Chapter 1

Christmas past was a disaster, a complete and utter waste of a perfectly good day. Christmas present promised to be no better, at least as far as Jeffrey Carston was concerned.

He sat in his office, pencil in hand and nose to the ledger, his only light the faint yellow glow of a twenty watt lamp, bright enough, he thought, to finish his work; dark enough to avoid detection by the world outside his window.

From Jeffrey's appearance, you would hardly guess that he was only thirty-three-years-old, let alone the president of the savings and loan: His face was drawn, his blue eyes burned red, his brown hair hinted of gray, and his suits, though freshly pressed, fit a heavier build.

When the final entry was made, he leaned back in his chair and sank deep into its comforting arms. The scent of his father's favorite tobacco still haunted the inner recesses of the soft, leather cushions. Jeffrey inhaled the aroma as if it were the elixir of life. He looked at his father's portrait on the wall, smiled, and then pictured him in heaven--a rotund angel with small wings, a pipe fixed firmly between his teeth, and a halo of smoke swirling madly above his bald head. Jeffrey wondered if his father's angelic robes had pockets filled with butterscotch candy. He figured they did.

Three sharp raps sounded at the window. Jeffrey slipped the ledger into the desk drawer, then swiveled the chair around to see who was there.

The sun was setting, the sky a palette of reds and yellows.

A voice called out, "Is that you in there, Jeffrey?"

Two cupped hands pressed against the glass, framing the eyes of an all-too-familiar face.

"Of course it's me, Paul," Jeffrey said. "Who else would it be? What do you want?"

"Nothing," he answered. "I was just walking by, and I thought I saw a light."

Jeffrey switched the light off. "Good-bye," he said.

Paul shook his head. "Are you going to the meeting?"

Jeffrey switched the light on. "Meeting? Today?"

"Yes, today," Paul replied. "Do you want me to stop by for you?"

Paul's breath fogged the cold glass. He wiped it clean with his hand.

"No," Jeffrey moaned. "I'll see you there. Maybe?"

"What was that?" Paul asked.

"I said, don't bother. I'll see you there!"

"You better not be late," Paul warned, "or there'll be hell to pay."

Jeffrey huffed. "So, what else is new?"

Paul shrugged and walked away.

Jeffrey reached into his vest pocket and pulled out his prized pocket watch. It belonged to his father, and before him, his. It showed the correct time, but no longer chimed. The watch was attached to a gold chain with a green cat's-eye marble fob--his championship cat's-eye marble. The fob, the chain, and the watch were reminders of his youth, his following success at the bank, and the tragedy that took it all away.

"Another day gone," he said, putting the watch back into his pocket, "and not a dime more to come of it."

He leaned forward, cradled his head on his arms, and fell asleep. The desk shook, the drawer slid opened, and the ledger flew out and crashed on the desk.

"More money! More money!" his father called out. "You need more money to pay everyone back."

"There's no more to be made!" Jeffrey answered. "No more, I tell you. Look for yourself."

"There's always more," his father argued. "So wake up and get back to work."

Jeffrey opened his eyes and wiped the sweat from his face. Someone called his name. He turned with a jolt.

The window was a sheet of radiant white light. Jeffrey shielded his eyes with his hand. His backbone tightened; his skin crawled as a ghost from the past took shape on the glass.

"Go away," Jeffrey gasped. "Leave me alone, or I'll call the sheriff."

"No need to get nasty," Paul said with a chuckle. "I only thought you might want to bring the statue to the meeting."

Jeffrey rubbed his eyes. His face was flushed.

"I might want to do a lot of things," he said, "but that's not one of them."

"Just a suggestion," Paul answered.

"One best kept to yourself," Jeffrey complained. "Good-bye!"

"See you later," Paul said.

Jeffrey turned away. His eyes focused on the words printed on the calendar--Peace on Earth, Good Will to Men.

He ripped the page off, revealing the words printed on the sheet below--Happy New Year.

"Says who?" he asked.

There was a song riding the night air, a Christmas carol to be exact--"Hark the Herald," sung by the stranger on a nearby mountain as he looked down at Mayfield.

Snow covered the ground and crowned the trees. The streetlights were decked with garland and wreaths. Silver bells jingled when shoppers entered the stores, while Santa, his reindeer and elves readied the sled in the square. It was a season's greeting image befitting a card, but the stranger was not.

He was lean and lanky and needed a good scrubbing. He was forty-years-old, his face was weathered, and his eyes were as black as the coal that gave the town life. He had bristly whiskers and long stringy white hair that stuck out like straw from beneath his pointed stocking cap. His clothing was like that of a soldier--a khakis uniform, a thick wool scarf that hung to his waist, and an overcoat that brushed the top of his leather boots.

All he possessed, he carried in a tote sack. His shelter was little more than a bird's nest, roofed with a tattered tarpaulin and bedded with rags and torn blankets--but the location suited him well. It was a short walk from town and provided concealment from meddlers and busybodies, the likes of which he found disturbing.

It was also an ideal vantage point from which to observe the comings and goings of everyone on the road below. The stranger's interest in people, however, was limited to the restaurant owner, who left pots of food on the back stoop for those in need of a meal; the sheriff, who was always on the prowl; a certain young girl, who was treated as an outcast, and the man for whom he searched.

The stranger bent over in pain. His stomach growled.

"Be quiet!" he ordered. "It's not time to eat!" But his stomach persisted and complained all the louder. He clinched his fist. "All right! Have it your way. I'll go to town. Now, silence your hunger."

A sudden breeze swirled around him. Its frozen fingers ran down his spine; its frosty breath whispered into his ear.

The man shivered. "It's a foul wind," he said, "that chills my bones and threatens the season. Take your lament to those who must listen," he argued, pointing to Mayfield, "and grieve me not."

He tossed his tote sack over his shoulder and hobbled down the path to the grotto below, dragging his right foot in the snow like a plow. When he reached the bottom, he walked over to a large bush and spoke to it without pause until interrupted by the sound of footsteps on the road.

The stranger turned. The bush shook, and some birds took flight.

"It's her," he said. "It's the girl in the paper." He pulled a newspaper clipping out of his coat pocket and waved it in the air. "Look for yourself if you dare. I told you I saw her, but you wouldn't believe me. Would you?" He looked at the girl and muttered, "But why is she out on a night like this?"

It was cold and damp, and the wind bruised the flesh as it rushed down the mountain to the valley below. He shrugged and put the newspaper clipping back into his pocket.

"One's in jail," he said, "and one's still free, but not for long," he promised. He tilted his head back and sniffed the air. "I know he's here; his stench lingers still." The stranger reached up as if plucking a star from the sky. "And when I find him, I'll take back what is mine and leave him to his grave." In his excitement, he skipped a step and tripped. The metal objects inside his tote sack clattered and clanged. He looked at the girl and headed for the safety of the woods.

The girl turned with a start to see who was there, but all she saw were two gray figures dissolve into the dark. At first she was frightened, but she quickly shrugged it off, saying to herself that it was nothing to worry about. They were, after all, running away and were apparently more afraid of her than she of them. She sighed in relief and continued her journey, but the road rumbled, and her flesh tingled. Something was coming.

Like the eyes of a cat, big and bright, the headlights of a car burst out of the night. The driver sounded the horn; the girl stepped back. The horn sounded again, but she had nowhere to go. The road was narrow, and the embankment was steep.

Her muscles tightened; she braced for the blow. But just when the car was about to strike, it swerved to the right and spun out of control, splashing her with a wave of slush and snow.

Head over heels, she tumbled and rolled all the way down the side of the road. When she finally stopped, she found herself sitting up, her hand scraped, and the package she carried lying in her lap. Then, just when she thought the worst had passed, the car door opened and a man got out holding what looked like a club.

His hot breath shot from his mouth like steam from a pipe. He raised his fists and cursed the person who had blocked his way. The last word spoken, he stomped the ground and walked to the front of the car.

The beam from the headlights bathed him in light. The shadow cast was long and wide. His face had an orange, jack-o'-lantern glow. He hammered the object he held against his glove-covered hand. It cracked with the sound of metal on leather. The girl squeezed the frozen package tighter and tighter until the brown paper wrapper crunched like ice, shattering the stillness and betraying her plight.

The man entered the shadows. He looked like a bear lumbering along in search of food, his weight shifting from side to side as he growled and slid down the side of the road.

The girl trembled and curled into a ball. The air was musty, darkness closed in. She thought all was lost, when the beam from a Ray-O-Vac flashlight pierced the night.

The man grumbled in an irritated tone and focused his flashlight on her face. She raised the packaged to shield her eyes. He let out a sigh, harsh and deep, and then pointed the light at her feet.

His hands shook; his voice had a quiver that betrayed his distress. She recognized him as soon as he spoke.

"What are you doing traipsing around out here at this time of the night, Mary Klein?"

The girl swallowed her fear and answered, "I'm running an errand for my mom, Sheriff Durben."

The sheriff growled to himself like a dog biting a flea on his rump.

"Running an errand?" he asked. "Out here? Now?"

His tone of voice let Mary know he didn't want an answer. He walked away, spoke to himself in a loud voice, and then returned.

Mary stood and brushed off her clothes. She appeared somewhat the vagabond. Her coat had seen more than its share of winters. Her black rubber boots were patched. Her dress was common. The wool pants she wore as leggings were thick, heavy, and baggy.

As for Mary herself, she was eleven-years-old, and, like her mother, had a scattering of freckles, deep-blue eyes, and long strawberry-blonde hair that fell just below her shoulders.

Sheriff Durben took the cigar out of his mouth, held the deformed stub of tobacco in front of his eyes, gave it a thorough inspection, then threw it to the ground and crushed it under his freshly polished shoe.

He wiped his lips with his sleeve and pointed his flashlight at the package in Mary's arms.

"Let me see that," he ordered.

She held out the package. He snatched it away in one, quick motion.

"What do we have here?" he said aloud.

He brushed the snow off the paper wrapping, exposing a name and a list of its contents (one hospital gown, one smock, two sheets and four pillow cases). He looked disappointed with his discovery.

"If this is for Doc," he said, snidely, "why didn't you take it to his office?"

Mary knelt and refastened the buckles on one of her boots, then the other. The sheriff thumped his leg with the flashlight, waiting for an answer. The beam bounced on the ground, up and down, faster and faster until she spoke.

"I went to his office, Sheriff Durben, but it was closed," Mary said, standing. "There was a note on the door saying that if anyone needed to see him, he would be at St. Andrew Church."

The sheriff gave the package back to Mary. He scratched his chin with his thumb and said, "So, Doc's at the church, huh?"

"That's what the note said, Sheriff Durben."

The sheriff spat a bit of tobacco out of his mouth and mumbled, "No doubt praying for another kiss from Lady Luck."

"What, Sheriff Durben?" Mary asked.

The sheriff answered, quick and smart.

"Nothing for your ears!" he replied.

Mary took a step back. The sheriff stepped forward and pointed his index finger at her.

"Make your delivery and go home," he advised, "and be quick about it!" The sheriff rubbed his neck. His face showed pain. "And watch out for vehicles on the road. I'm in no mood to write any accident reports tonight. Do you understand?"

Mary bowed her head. "I understand, Sheriff Durben."

The sheriff coughed. "Good," he said, clearing his throat.

A fresh cigar was quickly retrieved from his pocket, and a wooden match struck on his pistol belt. After the cigar was lit he took several long puffs and went back to his car without uttering another word. The incident was over in a matter of minutes, but to Mary it seemed an eternity. She didn't move a muscle until he drove away. Even then, her first step was long in coming.

St. Andrew Church was around the next bend in the road. Mary thought it looked like a castle. She imagined it was filled with knights in shining armor, protecting the town from the evil in the world. She tiptoed to the front door and cracked it open. The air inside was warm and inviting, but the words she heard were cold and sharp. They ricocheted off the door like spent bullets. The tone, if not the target, was all-too-familiar, so she closed the door and decided to wait by a nearby stand of trees for the doctor to come out.

# Chapter III

D r. Paul Bradford sat in his pew, listening to the chatter of the people and shaking his head in disbelief.

"Why isn't the statue here?" the choir director demanded to know.

She popped out of her seat like a Jack-in-the-box, flipped a lace-trimmed handkerchief in the air, and looked directly at Jeffrey Carston. Everyone between them moved out of the line of fire.

Jeffrey stood in response to the question, but directed his reply to Reverend Richmann.

"As you are aware," he said, clearing his throat, "the statue only arrived at my house last week. It's still in the shipping crate. I didn't plan on bringing it here until Christmas Eve."

Jeffrey turned to the choir director and mumbled something under his breath as he sat.

"Of course you didn't," the choir director argued. She had an accusing stare. "You always wait until the last minute to get things done. Why should this be any different?"

Dr. Bradford stood and straightened his tie. He was a handsome man and the only son of rich parents. He liked jeweled stickpins and cordial company, but most of all he enjoyed his profession.

"I don't believe that's quite fair," he said in a lofty tone. He stepped into the aisle and leaned aristocratically against the pew. "After all, the statue doesn't have to be in the manger until the day of the performance by our esteemed choir."

The doctor bowed to the choir, but the director crossed her arms and gave him the eye in reply.

"Some of us would like the privilege of seeing the statue before it's taken to the grotto. *After all*," she said, mimicking Paul's tone of voice, "we can barely see it from the choir stand that was built." She paused and tapped her foot on the floor. Everyone recognized the beat. "If you men had placed the stand closer to the manger like I *suggested*, we wouldn't be having this discussion."

The choir director ran out of breath and patience all at the same time. She looked at Dr. Bradford and sat, but he didn't look back. It was as if he feared turning into a pillar of salt.

Reverend Richmann cleared his throat in a manner meant to get everyone's attention. He was in charge when not forgotten. He was sixty-something-years-old, walked silently among those things worldly, and preferred to speak from the safety of the pulpit.

"I think we need to take a moment to reflect on the wonderful progress we've made. Everyone has worked hard to make our first living Nativity scene a success. And if we continue to work together, I'm certain everything will go smoothly."

His words flew through the church like a fly that everyone took turns swatting. The fly soon tired and met its end.

"I can keep the statue at our place," A voice cried out. "My husband and I have a perfectly good room in which to display it."

Jeffrey stood in defiant condemnation.

"I'm not taking the statue to any mortuary," he replied. "There's nothing wrong with it staying where it's at."

Reverend Richmann slammed his open hand down on the pulpit with a show of authority quite out of character. Everyone was amazed and momentarily stunned as he loosened his starched white collar, swallowed, and then spoke. "Since everyone is so adamant about seeing the statue before it's placed in the manger, I'll make arrangements to have it present inside the church during Sunday's service. That way, the whole congregation will have the opportunity to see it."

The reverend's words took everyone aback, but only a step or two.

"And, until then?" someone asked.

"Until then," Reverend Richmann replied, "Jeffrey can keep the statue at his house." Reverend Richmann forced a smile. "He can bring it here tomorrow afternoon while the choir is practicing."

"And then, what?" the choir director asked.

The reverend was about to answer, but Doctor Bradford stepped forward.

"And then, my dear," Dr. Bradford said, peeking at his wrist watch, "we all wait for Christmas morning and those inevitable lumps of coal. In the meantime, it's getting late, and we have one last issue to discuss."

Dr. Bradford motioned to Jeffrey. Jeffrey stood, tucked in his shirt, straightened his tie, and turned to the people for support before he spoke.

"As I told you last month, it was with great difficulty that I was able to get permission for us to use the grotto for our living Nativity scene and the Christmas Eve coral service. We all know the owner's attitude concerning any type of religious activity." Reverend Richmann frowned. A couple of the people muffled a chuckle. Jeffrey forced a smile and waited for the rest of the frozen faces to thaw before he continued. "Which is why I suggested at the last budget meeting that we purchase the grotto." Jeffrey paused and Reverend Richmann signaled for him to continue. "Well, three days ago, we closed the deal. The grotto is now ours, along with the surrounding four acres of land."

"Four acres!" a man yelped. "How much did that cost?"

Jeffrey adjusted his shirt collar and answered, "Five hundred and thirty dollars."

"That's a lot of money for that piece of land," the man replied.

"But it's well worth it," Jeffrey argued. "It's an ideal location for our annual picnic, not to mention a perfect place to hold special events." Several people voiced their agreement. Jeffrey took heart and continued. "As you know, it's just down the road from here and only a short walk from town. And now, because of the added acreage, everyone will be able to park in the open field instead of along the side of the road." Jeffrey paused, and a hint of a smile emerged. "I can also report that the construction crew I hired has completed their work on the manger and the choir stand. I even arranged to have some sheep and a donkey placed there to give the Nativity scene a more realistic appearance. Things couldn't be better."

Several people nodded their approval; whispers of support were heard. Jeffrey sat, his face aglow with pride. It was quickly extinguished.

"Hired!" the choir director shrieked.

The word echoed through the church like a thunderclap. It sounded as if the walls themselves were going to crack. Jeffrey looked at the ceiling as if hoping it would fall and end his distress before she continued. But it didn't, and she did.

"I thought you men were donating your time and energy? At least that's what you said."

"We were going to," Paul answered. He moved one pew closer to the exit. "Jeffrey and I were more than willing to organize the men and purchase the material, but everyone we asked to help with the manual labor said they were busy preparing for their own holiday activities. We had no choice,"

Paul said, waving his hands in the air, "but to contract the work and pay for it out of our own pockets." He paused and looked at his coat and hat lying in the pew. "Later," Paul quickly added, "we'll take up a collection to recoup our expenses."

"I certainly hope the collection compensates you for your efforts," the choir director said. "And compensates ours as well. We have new robes to pay for, remember." She paused for a moment, sprang from her seat, and pointed at Paul. "And I'm still not convinced the grotto is safe."

"Comes in threes," said an elderly man wearing a brown suit and clip-on bowtie.

His wife tugged at his sleeve and urged him to be quiet. Everyone within earshot turned to face him.

"The bank robbery last December," he said, counting one finger, "and the quake that followed," he said, counting another digit. "Sealed the grotto cave, it did, and a jug or two, I dare say."

His wife grabbed his hand and whispered, "A jug or two, huh?"

Paul cleared his throat in an effort to muffle a chuckle, turned to the choir director and said, "I don't think the new choir robes are in jeopardy. And, I might add, your concerns about the grotto were addressed to everyone's satisfaction by the mine's engineers at our last meeting."

Paul reached for his hat and coat. Jeffrey gave him a nod.

"I certainly hope you and those engineers are right," the choir director continued, "because we're the ones who are going to be singing on that stand *your* hired men built."

Reverend Richmann tapped his knuckles on the pulpit in an effort to get everyone's attention. Unfortunately, it sounded like a bird pecking wet wood and, therefore, wasn't immediately recognized. It took a more forceful effort to succeed.

"As Paul said, it's getting late. If you don't mind, we'll discuss the remaining church business after Christmas when everyone is in better spirit," adding as he eyed the side exit, "by the grace of God."

"We don't mind," Paul answered.

He signaled with his hat to Jeffrey and hurried to the front door. The reverend was left to fend for himself.

# Chapter IV

Paul stepped into the night. The wind howled as it rushed through the trees; clouds filled the sky, casting sinister shadows as they drifted across the face of the moon. Paul inhaled the air and filled his lungs. It was cold and damp, but strangely invigorating. He adjusted his hat and headed for his car.

"Wait a minute," Jeffrey cried out. Paul turned and buttoned his coat. Jeffrey gave him a queer look. "What's that pinned to your lapel?" Jeffrey asked.

"It's a sprig of mistletoe," Paul replied.

"You're not supposed to pin it to your clothes," Jeffrey said. "You're supposed to hang it somewhere in your house?"

"But there's no women at my house," Paul joked.

"Don't you mean woman?" Jeffrey asked slyly. Paul didn't answer. Jeffrey grinned. "Oh well, I guess holding it above her head will work just as well."

"I'll find out soon enough," Paul answered.

"I expect you will," Jeffrey said. "In any case, thanks for giving me a ride home. My wife apparently hasn't found the time to pick me up."

"Think nothing of it," Paul said. "No doubt she's doing some last-minute shopping."

"There's no doubt about it at all," Jeffrey complained. "I had a good look at her Christmas list the other night. It

stocked me, I tell you. I didn't know we had that many relatives still walking the earth. People seem to be living longer
these days."

"Happily, you're correct," Paul said, searching his pockets for his car keys. "Modern medicine made giant strides
during the war. I can't wait to start my surgical training and
become part of this new age of science  and technology."

"I'm glad one of us can't wait," Jeffrey said. He blew into
his hands to warm his fingers. "But I'm in a hurry, and it's
cold out here."

Paul heard footsteps and motioned for Jeffrey to stop.

"Look who's coming," Paul said.

He unlocked the car door and wiped the snow off the
window with his coat sleeve.

Jeffrey turned and grumbled, "Oh, it's her. Let's go."

"Nonsense," Paul answered. "We have a visitor."

"Your visitor," Jeffrey huffed.

Jeffrey got into the car, slammed the door shut, and
stared out the windshield, ignoring everyone.

A gust of wind caught Paul's brimmed hat and lifted it
from his head. Paul pursued and caught it at Mary's feet.

"What are you doing out here at this time of the night?"
Paul asked, cleaning his hat.

Mary's hair whipped across her face. Her eyes glistened.
Her cheeks were cherry red.

"Mom told me to deliver this," she said. She handed Paul
the package and stood straight and proud. "I went to your
office, but it was closed. The note on the door said that if
anyone needed to see you, you'd be here."

"So it does." Paul shuffled his feet in the snow. "But that
note was meant for emergencies. This could have waited until tomorrow or sometime next week. It's dangerous walking
this road in the dark, especially when the weather's bad."

Mary frowned. Paul gave her shoulder a gentle squeeze. Mary looked into his eyes and said, "Mom told me to collect one dollar and eighty-five cents."

"She did, did she?" Paul replied.

Mary held out her hand and waited for the money. Paul noticed the cut and examined it before she could protest. When he finished, he gave her hand a small pat.

"Make sure your mother cleans that cut with soap and water when you get home."

"I will, Dr. Bradford. May I have the money? If I'm not home when my mom gets back, she'll worry."

Dr. Bradford answered in a harsh tone that was as pretentious as his expression. "*No*, you may not have the money, Miss Klein. I won't allow you to carry it about in one of those coat pockets or in that injured hand. You might lose it on the way home. Then where would I be? We're talking about one dollar and eighty-five cents." Paul guided Mary to his car with a gentle hand to her back. "Do you know how many times I have to laugh at a patient's jokes to collect one dollar and eighty-five cents? Not to mention taking a chicken in trade." Paul opened the rear door and tossed the package inside. Mary looked at him somewhat stunned and confused.

"Go ahead and get in," he said. "I want to make sure that money gets to your house, safe and sound."

"But, Dr. Bradford, my clothes are wet. And my boots are covered with ice."

"No arguments," he answered. "And don't use your coat sleeve to wipe your nose. Here." He handed Mary a white, cotton handkerchief the size of a pillowcase. Mary blew hard. Paul took a step back, saying as he closed the door, "Keep it, with my compliments."

Paul inspected his new 1947 Chevy as he walked to the driver's side door. When he saw that the car was as pristine as the day he bought it, he brushed the snow from his coat, tapped the slush from his shoes, and proudly took his seat behind the steering wheel.

Mary wiped her nose, then neatly folded the handkerchief and tucked it away in her coat pocket.

Jeffrey shook his head and cleared his throat in a grumpy tone as he turned to Paul.

"I suppose this means I'm going to get home late?" Jeffrey asked.

"According to my father," Paul answered, "you were late when you were born."

Paul started the motor, looked into the rear view mirror, gave Mary a wink, and slipped the car into gear. As they drove along, Jeffrey voiced his complaints about giving her a ride. Paul said nothing in reply; Mary sat, emotionless. Her eyes focused on the floor.

"What's that?" Jeffrey asked. He turned in his seat and looked out the back window. "There's someone on the side of the road. See him?"

Paul looked into the rear view mirror. "I don't see anyone."

"He's not standing in the middle of the road, waving at us," Jeffrey replied sarcastically. "He's back by that stand of pine trees."

Paul moved the rear view mirror around to get a better view.

"I still don't see anyone. Are you sure it wasn't your imagination? Things look different at night, you know."

Paul gave Jeffrey a queer look.

Jeffrey's eyes narrowed.

"It wasn't my imagination," Jeffrey insisted. "I don't have an imagination according to you. Someone was there, and he definitely didn't want to be seen." Jeffrey paused and scratched his head. "Maybe it was one of those tramps from the railroad yards?"

"That's possible," Paul said. He placed the rear view mirror back into its original position, observing Mary's reflection as he did. His tone of voice saddened. "I'm afraid there are a lot of lost souls these days roaming the country since the war ended. They mean no harm. All they want is a few days work and a hot meal before heading on to God knows where."

"No sense crying over them," Jeffrey replied. "There's plenty of work to go around. We lost a lot of boys fighting those Nazis. The economy needs every able-bodied man to pitch in and help carry the load. It may as well be those hobos, tramps, or whatever they're called."

"They're called people," Paul answered.

The tires crushed the ice and slid in the snow as the wheels fought to follow the ruts in the road. Every now and then, Jeffrey glanced at Mary over his shoulder, saying something under his breath for Paul's consumption. Paul ignored the remarks and concentrated on his driving. The road was wet and slippery and filled with ice-covered potholes that could swallow a tire in the blink of an eye.

"Here we are," Paul said. He parked in front of Mary's house and turned around in his seat to talk to her. "Tell your mother that in the future, either I or my nurse will pick up the laundry for the office."

"Yes, Dr. Bradford. I'll tell her."

Mary tried to open the door, but it was frozen shut.

"Let me help you with that," Paul said, getting out of the car.

Paul gave the door a tug. It opened with the sound of cracking ice.

Mary looked at Jeffrey and said, "Good-bye, Mr. Carston."

Jeffrey leaned back and let out an audible huff in reply. Paul gave him a hard look as he extended his hand to Mary.

"Thanks for driving me home, Dr. Bradford. It was real nice riding in your new car."

Mary walked to the sidewalk. Paul took a deep breath.

"One minute, Miss Klein," he said, closing the car door. "Haven't you forgotten something?"

Paul crossed his arms and waited for a reply. She gave his question some thought and checked her pockets.

"The money," she said. "I forgot the money."

"Indeed you have," he said. "Come back here and hold out your hand. No, the one without the scrape." Paul reached into his vest pocket and pulled out a crisp five-dollar bill. "Give this to your mother."

He placed the money into her hand and closed her fingers over it.

"All of this?" Mary asked.

"Unless you have change in your pocket," he said jokingly. "Tell your mom it's a bonus in appreciation for her hard work."

Mary lifted one finger to examine the money. She had never held a five-dollar bill. Paul put his hand on hers, and she looked up. "And wish your mother a Merry Christmas for me," he added, cheerfully.

"I will, Dr. Bradford."

Mary held the money so tightly that she almost squeezed the ink out of the paper. She was at the front door when Paul told her to stop. His voice was stern, but he struggled to hold back a smile.

Mary turned.

"Did I forget something else?" she asked.

"You most certainly did. Come back here and hold out that hand again." Once again Dr. Bradford reached into his vest pocket. He pulled out a silver dollar and slipped it under Mary's clasped fingers. "That's for you," he said. "Mind you, it's not for candy, though I won't say you can't spend a penny or two on such things. However, I prefer you buy a heavy pair of mittens to protect that cut hand. Let's call it a prescription."

"A <u>persniption</u>?" Mary asked.

Mary looked at Dr. Bradford, her tongue unable to untangle the word.

"Close enough," Paul answered. "You better go inside before I have to treat you for pneumonia."

Mary grimaced and said good-bye. When Paul returned to the car, Jeffrey looked at his pocket watch to check the time, then closed it with a click and slipped it into his pocket.

"You should have kept that money," Jeffrey said. "You're going to need it tonight, if I know Sheriff Durben."

"It never rains on the righteous," Paul said, starting the car's engine.

"It's winter," Jeffrey answered. "And it snows on everyone."

Paul looked back to make sure Mary was safely inside. He remembered where she used to live--the white, Cape Cod on Willow Street. Mary's mother Cynthia had a flower garden in front. Mary had a playhouse in the backyard and a tire swing hanging from the limb of a large sycamore. Her father Sylvester spent the warm summer evenings on the front porch reading the newspaper and rocking in his favorite chair. Now, Mary and her mother were relegated to the confines of a three-room addition to a hardware store with no patch of earth to plant flowers, let alone a tree from which to hang a swing or a front porch to place a rocking chair.

Paul shook his head and switched on the radio. "Comes Love" was playing. Artie Shaw was his favorite bandleader and clarinet player; Jeffrey preferred Benny Goodman, another flaw in judgment that Jeffrey pointed out, and Paul ignored. When they reached Jeffrey's house, Paul steered the car into the circle drive, then stopped momentarily to admire the house before continuing.

The Carston house was one of the oldest and finest in the county and was situated in the nicest part of town. It was two-stories of sculptured stone and brick with two masonry fireplaces, one on each end of the house, that were like book-ends supporting a series of Gothic novels.

"Here you are, home sweet home," Paul said.

A Christmas tree was visible in the parlor. The front door was decorated with a wreath upon which was written in large, gold letters *Merry Christmas*. For an instant, Paul pretended it was his house. The only things he would have changed were the ornaments on the tree and Jeffrey's mood. He preferred more tinsel and less gloom.

"Thanks for the ride," Jeffrey said. "Tell Sheriff Durben hello for me."

"I will. Should I tell him you'll be there next week?"

"If my wife doesn't spend all my money," Jeffrey said, opening the car door.

Paul grabbed Jeffrey by the arm. "Wait a minute," he said.

"What?" Jeffrey asked.

Paul leaned back in the seat to gather his thoughts. Jeffrey looked at him, eyebrows raised.

"How long have we been friends?" Paul asked.

"I don't know," Jeffrey answered. "Five, six years?"

"Closer to ten," Paul replied.

"So?" Jeffrey asked.

"So, as your friend and family doctor, I guess I have the right to ask what's wrong."

"What do you mean? Jeffrey asked. "There's nothing's wrong with me," he insisted.

Paul looked directly into Jeffrey's eyes and said, "I'll say it plain and simple. You haven't been yourself since the robbery."

Jeffrey took a deep breath. "You and my wife," he said, shaking his head. "I told her, and I'm telling you. I've been busy, very busy. You know, working."

"No. It's more than that. You've always worked hard, but you never let it affect your personal life." Paul gave him a pat on the shoulder. "It's the robbery. I know it. You and this town, it's all the same. You can't forget; you can't forgive. It's like a festering wound that everyone keeps scratching." Paul leaned back in the seat. "Well, old friend, it's time you let go. It's time this whole town lets it go before it destroys everything we cherish in Mayfield."

Jeffrey sighed, and then said in a calmer voice, "It's not the robbery."

"Then, what is it?" Paul asked.

"It's Dad," Jeffrey said. "If he had been there, things would have been different." Jeffrey hesitated. "He wouldn't have let it happen. He would have done something."

"Done what?" Paul asked. "Get everyone killed?"

"No," Jeffrey replied. "Take care of business. I should have transported all that cash to the state bank. He would have. He would never have allowed that much money to lay around in the vault."

"Maybe? Maybe not?" Paul said. "But you don't know that; no one does."

"I do," Jeffrey said. "I let him down; I let everyone down."

Jeffrey's eyes watered. He opened the door and slammed it shut. His footsteps were slow and deliberate as he walked to the house, even though the driveway and sidewalk were clear of ice and snow. It was as if he were a burglar who feared detection by the occupants.

Paul shook his head and honked the car horn. Jeffrey jumped a foot in the air. When his feet returned to the ground, the house door opened, and Paul drove away.

# Chapter V

f you drew a line north from St. Andrew Church, it would follow the main road to the town square, pass through the park with its marvelous hill for sledding, then continue to a place packed with monotonous rows of identically constructed wooden frame houses, the railroad yard with its endless crashing and coupling of cars, and the coal mine, where the work whistles and black dust were constant reminders of the sacrifice required to put food on the table and clothes on the children.

The people who lived there were mostly Polish and Welsh immigrants who were married to the mine. Others were farmers and sharecroppers who were divorced from the land. Nestled in this part of the community was Mount Carmel Church.

It was originally built from logs, but later covered with broad-cut pine siding. It had a bell-less steeple and plain glass windows. The interior smelled of pine cones and needles. The front door was made of hickory and had a wooden cross carved in it. The cross was smooth and shiny from years of touching by those who entered. Other than this and a wonderful organ, the church had no remarkable or endearing characteristics whatsoever. It was nowhere near the size or grandeur of its rival, St. Andrew Church, but it did have a young and energetic pastor, Amos Weatherby.

He and Reverend Richmann were the crown jewels of Mayfield.

The two were close friends but voracious competitors for the souls of man, except on those rare occasions when they joined forces to thwart the advances of the dreaded Papist with the Irish accent, the circuit priest, Father Joseph Allen.

On this particular evening, various members of Mt. Carmel Church, like St. Andrew Church, had gathered for a meeting. Pastor Amos stood in front of the pulpit, implementing his role as mediator and *sayer* of the last word. His wife sat quietly in the front pew, watching him with admiring eyes as he paced the floor. Sitting next to her was the part-time church organist, Cynthia Klein.

Cynthia belonged to Father Allen's congregation. They held their service at the hall built by the Polish mine workers. They didn't have a real church to speak of or a full-time priest, let alone an organ, so she played at Mt. Carmel whenever she could.

"Before we end our meeting tonight," Pastor Amos said in a loud voice for the benefit of the people who had prematurely walked to the exit, "we have an issue that needs resolving."

Muffled moans accompanied them back to their seats.

"As I was saying," Pastor Amos said, staring at the nearly departed, "before we leave tonight, we have an issue to resolve--Santa Claus."

A woman stood and spoke the first words on the subject.

"Several of the parents want someone else to be Santa Claus this year, Pastor Amos."

A man turned to the woman and said mid-yawn, "I thought we settled that last year at the hall."

Pastor Amos took a deep breath, slowly releasing it before he spoke. "I know we voted to have someone else play Santa this year, but apparently no one bothered to inform Mr. Rosensky of our decision."

"Perhaps Father Allen could talk to him?" a man asked.

The man looked at Cynthia then at Pastor Amos as if imploring them to use their influence with the priest.

A hush settled over the small group. Pastor Amos rubbed his neck and took a step forward. Cynthia's face was flushed.

"Mr. Rosensky won't let us use the hall if he isn't allowed to be Santa," Pastor Amos said, "no matter what Father Allen says. Those Poles aren't going to listen to any Irishman, even if he happens to be, by some strange quirk of fate, their priest. I'm afraid our former arrangement with the lodge will have to stand, at least for the time being." Pastor Amos shook his head and walked over to his wife. "Rosey gets to be Santa, and we're stuck with it."

A mousy voice squeaked from a dimly lit area in the rear of the church.

"But it isn't fair. I know it's their hall, but we should be able to have our own Santa this year. I don't think that's asking too much."

Pastor Amos squinted.

"Is that you hiding back there, Honeycut?" Pastor Amos asked.

"It is," he answered, lowering his voice to a more manly level.

"Then you should know better than most. You work with him," Pastor Amos said.

"I still don't think it's too much to ask."

Honeycut slid down in the pew until only the top of his head was visible.

"If you're Rosey it is," Pastor Amos' wife replied.

Several of the women giggled. The pastor tried without success to keep a straight face.

"We must remember," Pastor Amos said, "that Santa isn't what's important." He tilted his head skyward as if reading words written on the ceiling. "It's Christmas, the birth of our Lord and Savior. Hallelujah!" Pastor Amos raised his arms in the air and shouted, "Glory be to God!"

He turned with a jerk and headed for the pulpit. His wife coughed and cleared her throat. He paused and walked back to the pews.

"We must keep in mind," Pastor Amos said, "that there are families in our community who need our help. Their children won't care who plays Santa as long as he has a gift for them. A gift they would not otherwise receive."

Pastor Amos paused to gather his thoughts. He stood in front of his wife and Cynthia. He put his hands on the pew and bent over, speaking slightly above a whisper. Everyone leaned forward to hear what he had to say.

"As I told you last Sunday, there's going to be a miracle." He suddenly shouted, "Hallelujah! A miracle of joy and hope this Christmas." Everyone snapped back in the pews as he raised his arms in the air and spoke. "I've seen it coming like a light in the night. I can't make it out, but I know it's there. When it arrives this Christmas, it will be as thunder from Heaven. The ground will shake and the mountains will tremble." Pastor Amos pointed to the people in a sweeping motion. "Truth will stand on the shoulders of the wicked and shout repentance into their ears. It will enter the hearts of the righteous and make them Lions of the Lord. Amen!"

Everyone answered, "Amen!"

Pastor Amos would have continued, but it was getting late. He could tell that it was late because one of the men was stretching and yawning. This particular man was his unofficial clock. He would stretch, yawn, close his eyes, fall asleep, and finally bump his head on the pew. The reverend therefore relented and turned to Cynthia, not wanting to be the instrument of pain to a member of his flock.

"Cynthia Klein!" Pastor Amos said. His voice was still alive with excitement. It caused Cynthia to sit erect. "I wish to personally thank you for your time and talents. In your inspired hands our organ truly possesses the keys to heaven. I thank you for being such a good friend to our congregation.

I have talked to the members of the choir, and like me they have only the highest regards for you. Because of your playing and their singing, I know our Christmas Eve service will be an inspiration to all who attend."

Cynthia blushed. "Thank you, Pastor Amos. It's a joy to play such a marvelous instrument, and I thank you for allowing me the privilege of accompanying the choir during the Christmas Eve service." She paused and looked down at her folded hands. "I also apologize for Rosey's stubbornness."

"No need to apologize," Pastor Amos said. "We all know Rosey has a good heart. A misguided one perhaps, but a good one all the same." Pastor Amos smiled. "Before we leave, I have some good news to share. There will be no more cold meals or burnt hands from carrying all those hot pots to the hall the day of the service. The hall now has a cook stove of its own." Everyone applauded the news, but before any comments could be made, Pastor Amos continued. "Also, some of our men have once again volunteered to take the organ over to the hall." Some chuckles were heard, but he ignored them. "I thank them and their strong backs, and I thank every one of you here for your efforts. They will surely be rewarded."

A few of the people wanted to resume the discussion about Santa, but the reverend stopped them by raising his hands and closing his eyes, signaling that he was finished, and now it was the Lord's turn. "Let us pray for the success of our Christmas Eve service and the safety of everyone here as we walk home on this dark, dreary night. Dear merciful and loving God..."

# Chapter VI

"Three aces!" Dr. Bradford cried out. He slapped the cards down on the table. "Read them and weep."

Sheriff Durben and two other men, one bald and one bearded, mumbled their complaints.

"That's four hands in a row you've won," Sheriff Durben said. He took the cigar out of his mouth and pointed it at Paul. "Maybe I should arrest you."

"For what?" Paul asked.

"For having too much luck for one human being," the sheriff replied.

The sheriff didn't like losing at anything, particularly poker--his second love in life. To make matters worse, he had recently celebrated his fiftieth birthday and was taking it out on everyone he knew. The sheriff, however, neither looked his age, nor acted it at times. He was of medium height, two hundred pounds; had brown eyes and short, brown hair. He smoked dime cigars down to the stub and occasionally visited the state capital for a taste of the night-life. He didn't have a steady girlfriend. He couldn't handle personal commitments, and, as he often commented, he didn't see any reason to prove it by getting married and mak-ing someone miserable ever after. He knew everyone in Mayfield by first name, especially the good ones, and watched over them all like a father, particularly the bad ones.

"If I were you, Sheriff," Paul said, counting his winnings, "I'd ask for a raise. Pickings are getting pretty slim."

The man with the beard shook his head and put the remainder of his money back into his pocket.

"I've had enough fun for one tonight," he said.

The bald man threw his cards to the middle of the table, counted the change in his hand, and dropped it into his shirt pocket.

"My wife's going to skin me alive when I get home," he said, pulling out his pocket watch. "I'm three hours late and twelve dollars short. Too bad Jeffrey couldn't make it. We could have used some of his money."

Sheriff Durben grabbed his few remaining coins from the table and dropped them one by one into an empty quart mason jar.

"Forget about Jeffrey," Sheriff Durben said, examining his depleted jar of poker money. "I can do without looking at that sour face. He hasn't been the same since the robbery. I don't think he will ever get over it."

"Who will?" the bearded man replied.

Paul stopped counting his winnings and looked at the man with the beard who, in turn, scratched his hairy cheek like a dog a collar.

"A lot of people are still trying to get over the bank robbery," Paul said. He carefully folded his winnings, and then put the money into his pocket. "A few more nights like this and that ring will be paid for."

Paul looked around hoping no one had heard him.

The sheriff bit down on his cigar.

"A what? For who?" Sheriff Durben asked.

"You never mind who," Paul answered. "You have more important things to worry about."

"Like finding the bank money I suppose?" Sheriff Durben replied.

His voice was bitter; his eyes opened wide. He slapped his hand on the table and everyone jumped.

"What brought that on?" Paul asked. "We all know you did your best to find the money."

"Well, I don't," Sheriff Durben said. "There's always something more you can do." He looked at the two men, and they faced the door. "I think it's time I paid Sylvester another visit at the state prison," Sheriff Durben said. "During my last visit I asked him to come clean and tell me who his accomplice was so we could recover the bank money and the mine payroll. But the fool kept professing his *innocence*." The sheriff nearly spit the cigar out of his mouth when he spoke the word. "I guess he thinks his accomplice will save him his share of the loot. Well, I'm saving something for him. I only hope I get the chance to give it to him when he gets out."

Paul stood, adjusted his tie, and tucked in his shirt. He patted his pants pocket in search of his car keys. The change in his pocket jingled. The sheriff turned and gave him the eye.

Paul replied, "You know what I said at the trial about the handcuff marks on his wrists?" As Paul spoke, the other men got their coats and moved closer to the door. "To my way of thinking it added weight to Sylvester's story and should have been given more consideration."

The sheriff took the well-chewed cigar out of his mouth and spat a bit of tobacco to the floor before speaking.

"He could have received those marks anywhere. I was so angry I could have given them to him myself when I arrested him. You know that."

The sheriff stood and kicked the chair into the table, tipping over his money jar.

Paul took a deep breath, hesitated, and then said, "All I know is what Sylvester testified to under oath."

"Under oath," the sheriff snickered.

The sheriff walked over to Paul and stared at him for a moment before he spoke.

"I suppose you believed that cock-and-bull story of his about being kidnapped by a stranger, forced into the vehicle at gun point, handcuffed to the steering wheel, and then made to drive the stolen getaway car." Sheriff Durben took a step back and rolled the cigar in his mouth like a peppermint stick before continuing. "And during all that time good ole Sylvester never saw the bank robber's face, except, of course, for those gold teeth he said the man had."

Paul calmly answered, "He did say the man never took his bandana off except for that one time he raised it to spit. In fact, neither Jeffrey, his clerk, or Reverend Richmann could give you a good description of the robber. As for the rest of Sylvester's story, I don't know if I believe it or not." Paul walked over to his coat to search for his car keys and make his escape. "But you did find the getaway car outside of town, and it was reported stolen from Turpin's gas station."

Sheriff Durben replied in a rough tone. "I found the car, all right. But it was hugging a tree, if you remember. And no one was there except Sylvester slumped over the steering wheel, unconscious and bare-<u>wristed</u>."

"Sylvester explained all that," Paul said.

Paul grabbed his coat and shook it. The car keys rattled, and he took them out of the pocket.

"He explained a lot of things," the sheriff replied, "but none of his explanations could be collaborated by evidence or witnesses. I particularly liked his story about deliberately crashing the car on purpose to prevent the robber from getting away with the town's money." The sheriff tilted his head back and rolled his eyes. "I don't think so. He wanted to ditch the car where no one would find it, and blew it. It's as simple as that."

The sheriff lit a match and tried without success to re-light his cigar. Angrier, he threw the match to the floor, stomped on it, and then walked over to the door, positioning himself so each of the men would have to pass him as they made their escape.

Paul put on his coat and hat and went to the door. The other two men followed.

"One day I'm sure the truth will come out," Paul said.

He patted the sheriff on the arm as he and the other two men passed.

"One day my foot!" Sheriff Durben shouted from the doorway. "It's already been a year!" The sheriff threw his cigar at Paul. Paul ducked and quick-marched to his car. "I'm going to get Sylvester's accomplice," Sheriff Durben shouted, "and recover the money, and it won't be *one day*."

# Chapter VII

Saturday morning found the sledding hill in the park covered with children. The weather was perfect, and the children were filled with energy.

A few of the children had store-bought sleds with steel runners, moveable rudders for steering, and hardwood decks. The riders called them "belly busters." Other children had homemade sleds crafted from discarded mining equipment crates; some had runners, but most did not. The sleds that didn't were more like toboggans that you pointed in one direction and hoped for the best. The rest of the children slid down the hill on whatever they could find with a slick surface and room enough for their bottoms. Mary Klein, wearing a cotton dress over a sewn-to-fit pair of heavy, wool pants, fell into the latter category. Her sled consisted of a waxed cardboard box courtesy of the butcher's trash bin. It was clean, but the aroma of roasts and steaks were still present, though unrecognized by the rider. Her only concern was making the box last a full day's sledding before it came apart at the seams.

Some of the boys were having a contest to see who could come closest to the large oak without crashing. The tree apparently had had the audacity to plant itself in the middle of this winter's sled run. It now paid the consequence.

Toby Carston, regarded by many as the best sledder in Mayfield, was ahead in the contest. He had a scraped knee, a bruised elbow, and his own cheerleader, Mary Klein. Toby (three months and ten days older than Mary, as he often reminded her) had dark-blonde hair, gray eyes and stood a head above the rest his age. Mary thought him quite the man in his brown corduroy pants, Navy P-Coat, and red stocking cap, but to her dismay, he was only interested in the glory of victory as he anxiously waited at the bottom of the hill for his nemesis, Bailey, to plunge toward the tree on his new Western Flyer sled.

On Bailey's previous run, he was an inch shy of taking the lead. This would be his last attempt for the day, so he examined the slope with all the care of the county surveyor. He pointed to the oak, sighted down his arm like a rifle and mapped his course, noting every bump, and memorizing the location of every rock and hard patch of snow and ice.

When the task was done, he lowered his arm and smiled ominously at Toby, who lifted his chin nonchalantly and turned to the tree. Whereupon, Bailey grabbed his sled, ran to the edge of the hill, and jumped into the air like a bird taking flight.

He was a quarter way down when his sled hit the ground, throwing snow in every direction. But Bailey held on tight, his belly glued to the sled, and his fingers firmly fixed to the rudder.

Onward he raced, his sled twisting and grinding and leveling everything in its path, until all that stood between him and victory was one last mound of rock-hard ice. He lowered his head and slammed into it, shattering the mound to bits. But when he looked up, he was a foot off-line and heading straight for the center of the battle-hardened oak.

The onlookers yelled, "Look out! You're going to crash!"

Bailey pulled the rudder as hard as he could, but it was too little too late. The knight on the wooden chariot had fallen to a superior foe. Bailey's sled and pride lay battered in the snow for all to witness. Toby retained his throne. Bailey was crowned, his head cut, but otherwise unblemished. It was a noble wound worthy of the care of a fair young maiden or, in his case, a complaining mother.

Bailey examined his sled. The paint was scratched, but other than that there was no visible damage.

"You better go home," the children advised, "and have that cut on your head looked after."

"I'm all right," a heroic but slightly dizzy Bailey told them. He placed his gloved hand over the small cut to stop the bleeding and turned to Toby. "By my count that makes us even. Tomorrow it's one run, winner take all. Agreed?"

"Agreed," Toby said. "Tomorrow one run for the world championship."

Toby cocked his head in a show of confidence. Bailey, sled rope in hand, gave it a tug and headed home, walking tall and exhibiting as much dignity as he could muster.

Toby placed his foot heroically on his sled as if posing for a portrait. Mary stood next to him, her big blue eyes blinking like Christmas tree lights.

"You made a wonderful run today," Mary said.

Toby took a deep breath, and then let it out in one gush.

"Tomorrow," he said, "me and Old Red are going to become the undisputed world champs." He bent down and wiped the snow off the seat of his faithful steed. "No one can defeat me and Old Red."

"No one," Mary replied.

She took hold of the cardboard box she used for a sled and headed for the top of the hill for one last run before going home to start her chores. Toby walked by her side. Every now and then, she turned to him and smiled. He gave her a quick glance in reply. When they reached the top of the hill, Mary let go of the box and looked with envy at Old Red.

Toby pulled the sled closer to his side. Mary lowered her head and nudged the box away with her foot.

"Would you like to slide down the hill on Old Red?" Toby asked, reluctantly.

"Do you really mean it?" she said. "Cross your heart and hope to die?"

"Of course I mean it. I said it, didn't I? I'm sure Old Red won't mind. He knows you well enough." Toby positioned the sled so it pointed downhill and extended a hand to Mary. "Here, let me help you get on. Now, this is what you do..."

Mary listened to every word. When his instructions were finished, he told her to hold on tight because Old Red wasn't accustomed to strangers; then he pushed her to the edge of the hill, where on the count of three, he gave her a shove that sent her flying down the slope faster than she had ever experienced in a butcher's meat box.

Onward she raced toward the oak. She held on with all her strength and steered the sled with the skill of a seasoned expert. Her heart pounded. The sled skipped across the snow like a flat rock on water, but Old Red held his course. Only twenty feet separated the sled and the oak. When ten feet remained, Mary pulled the rudder hard to the right and zipped past the tree, touching the trunk with her hand as she passed.

Toby ran down the hill.

Mary jumped off the sled and raised her arms in a cheer, "I did it! I did it! I touched the tree." She turned to Toby. "That was better than anything. Did you see?"

She grabbed Toby by the neck and gave him a hug before he could react.

"I saw it," Toby said, prying her arms off.

He moved out of her reach and looked at the children on the hill. Mary stepped forward and handed him the sled rope. He snatched it away, making certain she didn't come within hugging distance.

"You did real good," Toby said. "One of the best rides I ever saw."

"It was nothing compared to yours," Mary replied, "but it was marvelous all the same."

"Maybe tomorrow after I win the championship, I'll let you ride Old Red again."

"You will?" Mary said.

"If Old Red's up to it."

Toby turned to the mighty oak, then looked at Old Red and sighed. The church bells tolled the hour. All the children counted the rings. The number of children who departed increased with each toll of the bell. At the count of twelve, half of the children were gone.

"I better leave," Toby said. "It's time for lunch, and my mom will be waiting."

He gave a tug on the sled rope and walked away.

"Wait a minute!" Mary said. She ran over to Toby, reached into her coat pocket, and pulled out a red, white and blue paisley print handkerchief. "A knight has to be given a good luck charm before the tournament."

She extended her hand, but as he stepped forward to take the handkerchief, she planted a kiss on his cheek before he could do or say anything in protest.

"Don't do that," Toby said with a cringe.

He wiped away her kiss with the handkerchief before anyone could observe it glowing on his face, then gave Old Red's rope a pull and headed home.

Mary waved good-bye and ran back to the hill to retrieve her cardboard sled. She wanted to take one last ride, but when she sat in the box, she changed her mind. It wasn't the same. She took a deep breath and sighed. The excitement of riding Old Red and kissing Toby made sitting in the box seem silly.

She was about to leave when something flew past her ear. Bits of snow struck her head. She turned. A group of children called her name, and then a shower of snowballs rained on her like hail.

Mary jumped to her feet, held the box over her head and ran down the hill for the safety of the woods. The children pursued and continued the barrage. The box grew heavier with each hit. Snow brushed her face and burned her eyes. She was a few feet from freedom when a snow-covered rock struck her leg and she fell, re-injuring her hand and dashing any hope of escape.

She tucked herself under the box, like a turtle its shell, and sat helpless as the children circled. They drummed the box and mocked her in song. Mary didn't think it would ever stop, when suddenly it did.

The children were silent. Mary heard the shuffling of feet. Then one of the boys spoke. His voice was alarmed. "Something's in the woods," he said, "and it's coming our way." Another child replied, "It's an animal, maybe a lion. I've seen it here before, hiding in the trees and watching us with its big red eyes."

"There's no lions here," another boy said. "It's probably a haunt."

"If you're caught by a haunt," a girl muttered, "they'll put you in a pot and make soup."

Mary peeked out. A covey of quail took flight; a crow called a warning. Tree limbs cracked, the underbrush crunched. A gust of wind whipped through the pines and sprayed the children with ice. Then, a man popped out of a thicket, waving his arms and puffing air like a steam engine. He was big and scary and coming straight at them when the children scattered and ran back to the hill.

Mary pulled the box down tight and listened to the step drag, step drag rhythm of footsteps in the snow. Her heartbeat quickened with each step taken. Her muscles tightened. Seconds passed, and then a minute, and then another. She waited for the inevitable, but nothing happened. When she peeked out, no one was there.

Her body shivered. There was blood on her hand. She washed it away with some snow but refused to cry. She wanted to go home, but how? The children were on the far side of the hill. If she went there, they would renew their attack, and their words stung more than the snowballs. The railroad trestle was alive with empty coal cars traveling to the mine. They bumped and rumbled down the tracks like hungry beasts hurrying to a meal. The only way left was the path through the woods. She wasn't afraid of haunts. They were only stories made up by the parents to keep the young children out of the woods. So she threw the box off and ran as fast as she could. She didn't stop to catch her breath until she reached the other side. She was about to leave when something caught her attention--a man singing a Christmas carol.

"Dad?" Mary said with a hush. It was his favorite song, and it sounded like his voice. She stepped back into the woods and whispered, "Is that you, Dad?"

She wanted it to be him. She wanted to believe, although it couldn't be. The melody floated in the air like feathers on a warm summer breeze, soothing and hypnotic. Her fear left; her curiosity grew, and before she knew it, she found herself at the edge of a clearing, looking at a man seated on a log, staring into a campfire.

# Chapter VIII

t was like a dream. Icicles clinging to the branches collided in the breeze, then fell to the ground like autumn leaves. Snowflakes sparkled in the sunlight like diamonds. Thick, gray smoke rose from the campfire and swirled in the air. Embers popped while yellow and green flames pirouetted on a bed of simmering coals.

Mary smiled.

The man threw something into the fire. It exploded into a thousand darts of light. A bush rustled. Something in the shadows bolted and ran away.

Mary stepped back.

The man turned.

"Oh, it's you, Mary," he said. "Come over and warm yourself. No one here will harm you, my child."

His voice was comforting, but it wasn't her father. It was a stranger wearing an old army overcoat and a pointed stocking cap.

"How did you know it was me?" Mary asked.

The man ignored her question. Mary approached, but kept her distance, keeping the campfire and several feet of open space between them.

The man looked at her questioningly.

"You look confused," he said. "Were you expecting someone else?"

"I thought I heard someone I know," she answered.

"Baritones tend to all sound alike," he replied with a chuckle. "Come, sit by the fire," he insisted politely. He brushed the log clean with his coat sleeve. "Don't be afraid," he said. "I won't harm you. You're shivering, and I see a wound that needs mending."

Mary held out her hand.

"I scraped it yesterday," she said, "and hurt it again today, and now it's bleeding."

"I wasn't talking about your hand," he said. "Nevertheless, I'll see what I can do to make it feel better."

She walked over and sat by his side. She didn't know why she did it. She certainly knew better than to approach a stranger, especially alone in the woods. Perhaps it was the fire. It was warm and inviting, or perhaps it was the man himself. She felt secure in his presence. He had a kind face, a soothing voice, and, like her, she sensed he was an outcast.

"How did you know my name?" Mary asked.

"I know many people and many things," he said. The man walked over to a nearby stump and returned with a small, leather-like tote sack. "Show me your injured hand," he said, sitting down.

She held out her hand and studied his face as he examined her wound. His eyes, though dark and deep-set, beamed with emotion. His lips betrayed a smile. His face reflected the calming, candle-like glow of the fire. His hands were large and possessed great strength, yet gentle to the touch. His appearance and mannerisms begged countless questions. It was important she learn more about him, although she didn't know why.

He reached into the tote sack and brought out a small red bottle along with some gauze and tape. She wasn't quite sure what the bottle contained. Iodine, she thought. She disliked anything medical that wasn't served with a teaspoon of honey.

As he tended her hand, he hummed his tune. Mary closed her eyes. The man was full of cheer. Strange, she thought, for someone who seemingly possessed so little.

"Finished," he said with a smile. He placed everything back into his tote sack and rubbed his hands together over the campfire. "Does it still hurt?" he asked.

Mary inspected his work, flinching as she felt the bandaged cut.

"It hurts a lot," she replied.

"Good. If it hurts, it will heal. All things in pain will one day heal," he said, massaging his leg. He looked at her and sighed. "Then again, one day is much like another. Let's see what I can do for the pain."

He placed her injured hand in-between his and clasped them together as if in prayer. He blew into them, looked deep into her eyes, and then told her in a soft flowing voice that she had a little yellow bird trapped inside, and that when she opened her hand, the bird and the pain would fly away, and it did.

"Who are you?" Mary asked, feeling her cut hand.

He raised his arms in the air and shrugged.

"Who's to say?" he said with a cheerful voice. "Today, I am a caterpillar; tomorrow, a butterfly."

"What?" Mary asked.

She scooted a few inches away. The man recognized her fear and frowned.

"I didn't mean to frighten you," he said. "There's no cause for alarm, I assure you. Let's just say I'm a traveler taking the long way home."

The man was suddenly lost in his thoughts. Mary tried to get his attention by clearing her throat but failed. Finally, she said in a loud voice, "You never did tell me who you are?"

The man stared into the campfire. There was something in the ashes, a newspaper clipping. He grabbed a stick from the small pile of kindling next to his feet and pushed the clipping deep into the flames.

"I don't believe I'm a who," he said. "I used to be, or so I thought in my youth, but I'm older now and have my doubts." He rubbed his nose on his coat sleeve. "Perhaps I'm more of a what."

"A what?" Mary said. "That doesn't make sense."

"Well, you're a who," he replied. "And a very pretty who, I might add. But a what can be anything, perhaps one day even a who."

He bent over and sadness gripped his face. He sang his song and teased the flames with his stick.

"That's not right," Mary said.

The man looked at her and replied, "What's not right?"

"The words to the song," she said. "It's not *Angelo sings*, it's *angels sing*."

"Angelo?" the man said. "Are you sure I said Angelo? I could have sworn I said angels."

"No," Mary insisted. "You sang *Hark the Herald, Angelo sings*."

"Strange," the man said with a chuckle. "My name is Angelo. Maybe, I'm an angel. That would make everything all right, wouldn't it?"

Mary smiled.

"You can't be an angel," she said. "They have wings; you have a uniform."

"This uniform is only temporary," Angelo replied. "It will soon be shed. As for wings, not all angels have wings." He slapped his chest, then put his hand under his coat and scratched. "Although, a few of the residents residing within apparently possess them. At any rate, I imagine that wings would be awfully hard to keep clean. As for these clothes, usually a little soap and water will do." He stuck his nose beneath his coat and took a whiff, nearly falling off the log as he said, "Perhaps a mountain of soap and an ocean of water."

Mary put her hand over her mouth and giggled.

"I still think angels have to have wings," she said.

Angelo looked at her somewhat sadly then replied, "Your angel doesn't have wings."

"My angel?" Mary asked.

"Benjamin, of course," Angelo informed her.

Mary was stunned. Only she, her Mom, and her Dad called the angel that.

"Benjamin was my baby brother," Mary said with a frown. "He tore the wings off the Christmas tree angel, but he didn't mean to." The sadness faded and a grin took its place. "I guess Benjamin has his own wings now. How did you know?"

"Windows work both ways," he said with a wink, "and thin walls keep no secrets. As for Benjamin, he'll always be your angel." Angelo scratched his beard. His face grew stern. Mary sensed a change in mood. "Those children had harsh words for you," he said. "Did your father rob the bank and take the town's money?"

Mary's lips quivered.

"No!" she cried out. "He didn't do it!"

Mary took Dr. Bradford's handkerchief from her pocket and dried her eyes. Angelo peered into the fire and poked it angrily with his stick.

"I believe you," he said, "but the question had to be asked. From what I've read in the papers and heard in town, I thought as much." He threw the stick and some kindling into the campfire. He leaned back and crossed his arms, saying in an investigative fashion, "Did your father ever talk to you about the robbery?"

"He didn't talk to me much before the trial," she said solemnly. "Most of the time Mom and the lawyer spoke to him. I just sat and listened." Mary took a deep breath and grinned.

"But we talk now, whenever Mom and me visit him. Once, I even talked to him alone."

"Did he ever say anything about the bank robber?"

"What kind of things?" Mary asked.

"Things that could describe the man, like the color of his eyes and hair. Did he have a nose like an anteater and ears like an elephant?"

Mary wiped the tear from her cheek and smiled.

"Daddy never saw much of his face because of the bandanna, but he said the man had brown hair and green eyes and wore a hat."

Angelo scratched his beard.

"Your dad said that and more at the trial," Angelo mumbled. "Unfortunately, a lot of people have brown hair and green eyes and wear a hat," he said aloud. "Did your Dad say anything else?"

Mary gave his question some thought. She shook her head no, and then immediately changed her mind.

"The last time I talked to him, he told me the robber chewed a lot of gum. He stuck it on everything," she said with a shutter.

Angelo clapped his hands and rubbed them together over the fire.

"I knew it," he said, cheerfully. "If I'm correct, and I usually am, we are both seeking the same thief."

"Were you robbed, too?" Mary asked.

She wiped her nose, then folded the handkerchief and put it back into her pocket.

"I'm afraid I was," Angelo replied. "He took my wonderful astrolabe." Mary's eyes widened. Angelo leaned toward her and said, "When I find him, the truth will come out, and your dad will go free."

"Do you know who the bank robber is?" Mary asked.

Angelo turned away and massaged his leg.

"It's not time to reveal his name. If he escapes again, I may lose my astrolabe forever."

"You can tell me," Mary said. "I won't tell anyone. I promise."

Angelo patted her on the arm and smiled.

"I would shout it to the world," Angelo replied, "if my father was in prison."

Mary crossed her arms and gave him the eye.

"What's an astrolabe?" she asked.

"An astrolabe is a disc-shaped object about the size of a pie pan. Cherry, I think." He smacked his lips. "It was used by ancient astronomers to study the movement of the stars." Angelo paused. He heard a noise in the bushes, shook his head, and then continued. "I was told by Sipprus, the man who gave me that most marvelous instrument, that it once belonged to a powerful Magus." Angelo nodded. "Perhaps even to one of the Magi." Mary's face had a blank expression, but Angelo continued. "Sipprus taught me its secrets. On clear nights, I used it to find my way as I traveled from place to place. On special nights, I used it to read what was written in the heavens by all those tiny specks of light." Angelo looked up; his eyes twinkled. "The sky is like an open book; the stars are the words in that book. On those special nights secrets are told, and angels share stories of happiness and woe. But I fear people today bother not with such things. They never listen. To them, stars are only bright lights and," he said, giving Mary a gentle poke with his finger, "angels most definitely must have wings. And I suppose a who is no one, and a what...Well, we won't go into that."

"Who's Sipprus?" Mary asked.

"He was a remarkable man," Angelo said with pride. "We met in North Africa during the war. He saved my life and healed my wounds, much like I did yours." Angelo momentarily closed his eyes. "He was many things to many people, and a master of prestidigitation, I might add."

"Presti...what?" Mary asked.

"Magic," Angelo answered.

Angelo waved his hand in the air and produced a gold coin the size of a half-dollar between his fingers.

"Wow!" Mary said. "What is it?"

Angelo held the coin in front of her eyes, and then closed his fingers over it. When he opened his fingers, the coin was gone.

"Give me your hand," he said.

Mary held out her hand. Angelo tapped her palm with his fingers, and the coin reappeared.

Mary held the coin in the sunlight and examined it with care.

"It looks like a man with some weeds growing out of his head," she said. "And there's some funny writing on it."

Angelo smiled and said, "The writing is Greek, and the man is the Emperor Constantine. The weeds on his head," Angelo said with a chuckle, "form what is called a corona; it's a type of crown the Romans made from laurel leaves to celebrate a great victory or accomplishment, sort of a trophy you wear like a hat," Angelo said, grinning. "I've been told the coin is very rare and very valuable."

Angelo took the coin, waved it in the air, and it disappeared.

"How did you do that?" Mary asked.

"A magician never reveals his secrets," he said.

"Then," Mary asked, "how did you learn?"

Angelo leaned forward, tapped his index finger across his lips, and whispered, "There are exceptions to every rule. Otherwise, there would be no secrets."

Mary gave his words some thought, then asked, "Did Sipprus teach you?"

"Sipprus taught me many things before he died," Angelo replied. Angelo stared into the campfire. "He was killed. No. Murdered!" Angelo said accusingly. "And there was nothing

I could do to stop it. Nothing!" Angelo argued. "Absolutely nothing." He swallowed his anger like a bitter pill. There was a moment of silence, and then he spoke in a calmer voice. "I could feel his spirit leave his body as I held him in my arms and said good-bye. Part of him remains in me still and probably always will." There was a show of remorse in Angelo's face. It was contagious. Mary felt his pain. She wanted to cry, if not for him, then for herself. He brushed his fingers gently across her cheek. "You are young and full of life," he said. "Trouble yourself not with such matters. The burden is mine to carry."

Some snow fell from a tree branch. It landed in the fire, and the fire sizzled. Angelo and Mary smiled.

"I saw some men working at the grotto," Angelo said. "Do you know what they're doing there?"

"The men are building a manger and a stand for St. Andrew Church's choir," Mary answered. "The choir's going to sing there on Christmas Eve."

Angelo frowned. His voice was agitated.

"They shouldn't do that," he said. "Didn't you feel the tremor last night?"

"Tremor?" Mary asked.

"Earthquake," he said. "Twice in as many days. I had to move off the mountain for fear it would fall. That's why I'm camped here in the woods."

"I don't know anything about that," Mary said.

"Well I do," he said firmly.

A bush rustled. A loud whimper came from the direction of a nearby thicket. It startled Mary, but she hid her fear. Angelo ignored it completely.

"Didn't you hear that?" Mary asked.

"I heard it," Angelo said with a huff. "But it's just another *what* wanting to talk. A most annoying *what*, I might add. It follows me during the day like a shadow, and at night skulks about in the darkness like a spook. Ignore it and it'll go away."

The fire cracked. Angelo stirred the ashes with a stick and threw the stick into the flames.

"You must go," he said. He groaned and grabbed his leg. "The pain has taken control of my thoughts. Come back tomorrow."

Mary pleaded, "Will you tell me more about the bank robber?"

"Perhaps, tomorrow," he said, closing his eyes.

Mary stood and brushed the snow from her clothes. The Silver Star pinned to the lapel of her coat fell to the ground.

Angelo's eyes opened. He picked up the star and examined it.

"I've seen these before. Did this one fall from heaven?" he asked jokingly.

Mary smiled. "No, my dad gave it to me." She held out her hand and Angelo placed the Silver Star in her palm. "He got it in the war for being brave. When he came home, he had it made into a pin so I could wear it and be brave like him." She looked at it through watery eyes and pinned it back on her coat. "Mom says Dad is the only one in Mayfield with a Silver Star."

"Then, cherish it you should," Angelo said. "Now go. I have things to do."

"I'll see you tomorrow," she replied.

"I'm certain you will," he answered.

# Chapter IX

M ary cracked the door open and looked inside. Her mother was bent over the wringer washer. Her hair was wet, and her hands were covered with soapsuds. Mary held her breath and entered. The rusty hinges announced her arrival.

"Where have you been, Mary Elizabeth?" Cynthia asked. She wiped her hands on her apron and crossed her arms. "Did you forget I needed your help this afternoon?" Cynthia pointed to a stack of clothes in the corner. "Those shirts need to be ironed before the men get off work."

Cynthia brushed the hair away from her face with her fingers, leaving a large soap bubble on her forehead. Mary looked down so she wouldn't smile.

"I'm sorry, Mom. I was sledding on the hill with Toby and lost track of the time. I'll start ironing right away."

Mary kicked off her rubber boots, ran into the bedroom to change her clothes, and returned to begin her work.

"What's that on your hand?" Cynthia asked. She walked over to Mary. "Let me see it."

"It's nothing, Mom, really. I fell down, that's all."

"Fell down, huh?" Cynthia shook her head. "Did Toby's mother put this bandage on your hand?"

"No," Mary replied.

Her answer was faint. She turned her head to avoid looking into her mother's eyes.

"Then, who did?" Cynthia asked.

Mary hesitated but quickly relented when her mother crossed her arms and stared at her.

"It was a soldier in the woods by the trestle," Mary confessed. "He put the bandage on my hand." Mary paused. "But I did fall down."

"So you said," Cynthia replied. "Anyway, you stay away from the trestle. It's dangerous there. Only last month the Ramey boy fell off a moving coal car and broke his arm. Remember?" Mary nodded yes but said nothing. "Now, tell me more about the soldier who bandaged your hand."

"There's really not much to tell. He was tall, had white hair and wore army clothes."

Cynthia frowned and walked back to the washing machine.

"Probably just another veteran from the VA hospital in Charleston," Cynthia said.

"I guess so," Mary replied. "He didn't say."

Mary and her mother had met several veterans in the past who had been patients there. Sometimes they came to Mayfield by bus if they had money, or by foot or rail if they were broke. Some came looking for work at the mine; others were passing through on their way home. None of them had ever made trouble. In fact, Cynthia had even extended her clothes-washing services free of charge to several of them until they got on their feet or left town for parts unknown.

"Whoever he was, he knows how to make a bandage," Cynthia said, wringing the water out of a pair of pants. "Can you tell me anything else about him?"

Mary gave the question some thought as she placed the iron on the ironing board and plugged it into an extension cord that was half the length of the room.

"I think he was hurt in the war or something because he limped around on one leg. He has a beautiful singing voice," she said, adding cheerfully. "He's a baritone, like Daddy."

Cynthia smiled, and then hummed "Hark the Herald".

While Mary waited for the iron to get hot, she went over to the kitchen table to look at the Christmas tree. It was about two feet tall, too small to use for anything except a centerpiece. Cynthia had decorated it with some earrings that had belonged to her grandmother and a string of pearls that Sylvester had given her on their first Christmas together. Mary had made some ornaments in the shape of stars using cardboard wrapped in aluminum foil. But sadly, the porcelain angel looked out of sorts in its traditional place on top of the tree. It was, however, as beautiful as ever with its painted face and arms, golden halo, silver trumpet, and white linen robe, although as Angelo had said, it possessed no wings, thanks to Benjamin.

On one side of the tree there was a votive candle. On the other side, a gift for Mary and a small, wooden Nativity Scene. The crib in the manger was empty. Sylvester had baby Jesus with him in his cell. Mary secretly hoped the child would get lonely for his family and arrange for Sylvester to bring him home.

Mary waved good-bye to Benjamin and went over to the pile of clothes waiting to be ironed. Cynthia put another load in the washer and turned to Mary.

"In the future, you stay away from strangers. Do you hear me?"

"I hear you, Mom. But..."

"No buts, young lady."

"<u>Momm,</u>" Mary whined.

"You mind me. There are a lot of bad people out there; all smiles on the outside, but black as pitch inside." Cynthia wrung out a pair of socks with her hands, and then threw them back into the washing machine. "You don't know who they are or what they want, especially what they want."

A frown formed on Mary's face, but lifted as soon as she reasoned that Angelo could hardly be considered a stranger. They had already met, and he didn't want anything.

"What are we going to make for the community service on Christmas Eve?" Mary asked.

"If the butcher comes through with the ham bone, we're going to make a pot of bean soup."

"The kind with the big beans?" Mary asked.

"The same as always. They're in the pot now, soaking." Cynthia tugged at a sock stuck under the washing machine agitator. The sock snapped free, spraying soapsuds everywhere. Mary giggled; Cynthia smiled.

"When you're done ironing," Cynthia said, wiping her face, "remember to fold those shirts the way I showed you."

"I will, Mom."

Toby checked the garage to see if his dad's car was there, it wasn't. He didn't expect his dad to be home, but he hoped. When he walked into the kitchen, his mother Marge was in front of the stove, wiping her hands with her apron. He was late, but his thoughts were on the sledding hill several blocks away. He could have been home earlier for lunch if either his stomach had complained louder or the grocery store had been located in the opposite direction. But as it didn't, and it was, five cents of licorice and the upcoming championship slowed his pace considerably.

"It's about time you came home for lunch, young man," Marge said. "Didn't you hear the church bells?"

"I'm sorry, Mom. I had to clean Old Red. He had a hard day at the hill."

Toby rubbed his nose and sat down at the table.

Marge shook her head and grinned.

"If I didn't know better, I'd think you were born on that sled."

She opened the oven door to check the cherry pie she was baking. It and the other pies she had already baked were going to be a special treat for Christmas, provided she could keep everyone's fingers out of them.

She went over to the window, looked outside, and mumbled something.

Toby turned.

"What did you say, Mom?"

"Elves," she said with a smile. "I fear one of Santa's elves has gone astray and eaten one of my cherry pies. Either that, or I'm getting senile." Marge paused to give it some thought. "I could have sworn I set two sweet potatoes, one apple, one rhubarb, and..."

"Rhubarb?" Toby said with a sour face.

"For your Uncle Jed," Marge replied. "And two cherry pies. One for your dad and one for you." Marge smiled. "I put the pies on the stoop this morning to cool, and now I'm one cherry pie short."

Toby frowned.

"My pie?" he asked.

"Yours is in the oven," Marge assured him.

"Did you check for footsteps?" Toby said with a grin. "Elves have pointed feet."

"Of course," Marge replied. "But I dare say this particular elf has a limp and a four-legged accomplice."

"Is Dad home?" Toby asked.

"No," Marge said. "He had to take care of some last-minute business at the bank."

"But, it's Saturday. He promised to go sledding with me this afternoon."

"I wouldn't count on it. This is a busy time of the year for him."

Marge ladled some soup into a bowl and carried it over to Toby along with a measuring cup containing the leftover cherry pie filling.

"He's always working," Toby said. He stuck his finger into the pie filling, gave his finger a good lick, and then leaned over to smell the bowl of soup. "He doesn't want to do anything anymore except go to the bank."

"You shouldn't talk like that," Marge said. "It's just that at this time of the year, everybody needs him. And," Marge said, crossing her arms, "unless you're an elephant, you better use a spoon."

"Okay, Mom." Toby picked up the spoon and swirled the soup. "But he was supposed to be home early today. He promised."

"I'm sure he'll go sledding with you if there's time," Marge said, walking back to the stove. "Now, quit playing with your food."

"There won't be," Toby said solemnly.

Toby pulled out the handkerchief Mary had given him and wrapped it around his neck like a scarf. Whenever the soup dribbled down his chin, he mopped it up with the handkerchief.

"Where did you get that?" Marge asked.

"At the sledding hill," Toby said, reluctantly.

"Did you find it?" Marge asked.

"No. Someone gave it to me."

"Someone I know?" Marge asked.

"Yes." Toby looked at the stove. "Is there any more pie filling?"

"Afraid not," Marge said. "This someone wouldn't be Mary, would it?"

Toby didn't answer. Marge smiled, turned off the fire under the soup pot, and walked over to the table.

"She's a good girl," Marge said, running her fingers through Toby's hair, "and very pretty."

"I guess," Toby said, slurping his soup. "Didn't really notice."

"You will," Marge said, leaving the room, "sooner than later."

# Chapter X

While Cynthia and Mary labored over tubs of water, stacks of dirty clothes, and hot irons, a half-mile beneath their feet, men burrowed in the coal mines like moles in a hole. The shafts stretched like the tentacles of an octopus grabbing, scraping, and pulling in every lump of mineral needed to maintain its existence. As long as the monster was fed, the town survived.

Rosey stood in front of the engineering office, brushed the coal dust from his clothes and entered. He was tall, physically intimidating, had black hair, large gray eyes, and a clean-shaven face. A silver chain with a tiny silver bell was wrapped around his wrist like a watch. It used to be his mother's necklace. She gave it to him as a reminder never to raise his hand in anger. "An angry heart," she told him, "has no place in God's house."

"You sent for me, Mr. Daryl?" Rosey asked.

Mr. Daryl was examining something at a table. He turned, gave Rosey a hard look, and then said, "My general foreman calls me Steven, remember? The requirement comes with the paycheck."

Steven grinned, and Rosey breathed easier.

"The foremen are in the break room," Rosey said. "Should I get them?"

"No," Steven replied. "I want to talk to you alone. I have a problem to discuss." Steven motioned for Rosey to come over to a table in the middle of the room. The table had billing statements, drawings, and production reports spread out on it. "I need twenty-percent more coal production," Steven said. He picked up one of the reports, gave it a quick glance, and tossed it back on the table. "I have to increase coal extraction from shafts two and three."

Steven turned to Rosey for his comments. Rosey scratched his chin and went through the stack of orders on the table. He flipped through the production reports and billing statements. He studied the situation and considered alternatives while Steven paced the office and waited for him to speak.

"I don't believe you can get the increase you want with our present workforce and schedule," Rosey said. He leaned on the table and examined the work schedules. "The only possible way to do it is by having the men work overtime and by hiring some extra workers. I'm sure we can get a few of the old-timers to come back temporarily, but I doubt you'll be able to fill all these orders and show a profit."

"I thought about that," Steven said. "I'm willing to forego the profit if I can prevent my customers from buying their coal elsewhere. However..." Steven walked over to the table and shuffled through the papers until he found what he was searching for, a schematic of the shafts. "We might all be able to benefit if we reopen shaft number four," he said, pointing to the paper.

"Shaft number four!" Rosey replied. "That shaft has been nothing but bad luck since the day it was opened, and it continued even after the cave-in. The men don't like going anywhere near it. Some of them say they heard voices that couldn't have been scarier if the devil himself was calling out to them from the deepest pits of hell. Bill Luke swears he even heard a gunshot.

Men hear a lot of things," Steven insisted, "especially after a night out on the town." Steven looked at the schematic, folded it, and pushed it aside. "I need to reopen shaft number four. I have no choice." Steven paused. "Things have changed."

"Changed?" Rosey asked. "Changed in what way?"

Steven looked at Rosey and frowned.

"I had to borrow money from the State Bank in Charleston to meet next quarter's expenses and to buy some new drilling equipment, including a pair of those new, electric detonators you wanted." Steven turned away. "I could lose the mine if I don't reopen that shaft."

Rosey took a deep breath and leaned on the table.

"Then, I guess we'll just have to open that shaft."

Rosey looked again at the coal orders and production reports. They needed a lot of coal, more than they had ever mined in the past. He had his doubts they could do it, but if there were a way, he'd find it.

Steven leaned forward to study the work schedules.

"I know we can get that increase in coal output," Steven said in a reassuring tone.

"Of course we can," Rosey replied. "The crews will work long and hard, and not simply because of the extra money. They know what the mine means to the town."

Steven moved away from the table and placed his hands in his pockets as he paced the room. He had something to say, but was somewhat reluctant to do so.

"I want to blast shaft number four open, and as soon as possible."

"That's a risky proposition," Rosey warned. He turned to Steven. "Why not take a few days to clear it by hand and see what we have to deal with? There could be trouble on the other side of all that fallen rock just waiting for us to poke it with a stick of dynamite."

"We don't have the luxury of time, not even a few days. The bank wants its money in March, the Ides of March," Steven joked. Steven walked back to the table and stared at the papers. "I know you're worried, Rosey, but every precaution will be taken to protect the men, and no one except the blasting team will be allowed in the shafts at the time of the explosion."

"I still have my fears," Rosey said.

"I know," Steven replied, "but I need to get that coal."

Rosey circled the table, scratching the back of his neck as he walked. He knew what Steven wanted to hear, but he was concerned about the men and nothing was more important to him than that.

"I want to personally monitor and control the blasting," Rosey insisted, "and I want to call it off if there's any question of safety. Also, I'll want to make Honeycut the crew chief on the job. He'll complain, as usual, but he's the best driller we have."

"Agreed!" Steven said. "As of this moment, you're in charge of the work. If you want, I'll even give you my office." A faint smile appeared on Rosey's face. Steven sat on the edge of the table and breathed a sigh of relief. "All I want is to save the mine. As for Honeycut and the new work schedule, you can arrange it as you see fit."

"When do you want to do it?" Rosey asked.

"Christmas Eve," Steven said. "I'm afraid if we wait any longer and something goes wrong, we won't have enough time to initiate another solution. We'll detonate the explosives when the day shift is over, sometime after 5:00 in the afternoon. We'll clear the shaft the day after Santa's arrival." Steven smiled. "I certainly wouldn't want to interfere with that."

Rosey showed no expression. He looked at Steven and said, "I'll inform all the foremen and reschedule the crews." He walked over to the door, but as he reached for the doorknob he paused. "I just remembered." He turned and took a step toward Steven. His face showed concern. "Shaft number four runs under the grotto, doesn't it?"

"Not quite. It runs a little north of it," Steven answered. "At any rate, we checked the grotto area out a couple weeks ago and gave it a clean bill of health."

"A little north?" Rosey muttered. "A couple weeks ago?"

"You're getting nervous over nothing," Steven replied.

Rosey gave it some thought, then turned to leave.

"Merry Christmas, Steven."

"I certainly hope so, Rosey."

The break room door was closed. Rosey paused to listen to the discussion going on inside among the shift foremen before entering. Apparently, they all knew what was coming, and none of the foremen were in favor of changing the work schedule.

"Why not," Rosey said, entering the room.

There was a moment of silence.

"We worked hard for our seniority," one replied.

"I like the shift I'm on," another said. "So does my wife."

Someone laughed.

"Is this really necessary?" another man asked.

"It is," Rosey said. "We have to change the work schedule, but it's only temporary. Each of you will return to your regular shift after we fill the new coal orders."

"Change is never for the good, if you ask me," someone said. "Once you change something, you can't change it back."

"True enough," Rosey answered. "But the schedule will return to normal. Whether or not we are the same after this will depend on what we do now. In short, we have no choice. If we don't pull this off, there may not be a mine to come back to next year."

"We heard that we have to open shaft number four," someone asked. "Is that true?"

"True enough," Rosey answered. "It has to be done." The men complained. Rosey's voice hardened. "It's going to be done, like it or not. Mr. Daryl wants the charges set off on Christmas Eve sometime after five in the afternoon. Honeycut's crew will do the drilling; I'll set the charges myself. We'll clear the shaft after the Christmas holiday. As for the schedule, I'll post it in the morning." Rosey walked to the door, then stopped. He had one last thing to say. "It looks like Christmas is going to be our last day off for quite some time, so enjoy it. Just don't let me catch anyone stumbling in drunk the next day."

One of the foremen stepped forward; he didn't look happy.

"And I suppose New Year's is going to be dry as well?" he asked.

"Not with those tears, it ain't," Rosey replied.

# Chapter XI

The hands on the Dr. Pepper clock above the Kleins' cupboard marched to the hour of four. Mary was hunched over the ironing board. It had been a long, hard day, and every muscle in her body ached. She was completely exhausted, but she dared not stop. The shift change at the mine was approaching, and some of the men would probably stop by for clean work clothes. Mary wanted to be finished before they arrived so she could help her mom sort the clean clothes, tie them into bundles with string, and attach the bills.

Cynthia had already started the next day's wash. After ringing out the last pair of pants, she hung them on the line in front of the coal-burning stove to dry, and then drained the dirty wash water from one of the two wringer washers, one of which always seemed to be running. The water gurgled and bubbled out of the hose as it flowed into the sink and ran down the drain. Mary looked at her mother, draped over the washer like a dishtowel and staring into the swirling gray water.

A tear formed in Mary's eye. She wiped it away with her hand and hung the last pair of socks on the line by the stove.

Cynthia yawned, stood straight as a board, and stretched.

"Mary," she said, turning around, "I want you to take that bundle of clothes by the door over to Mr. Svezic's. He's been sick the past few days and couldn't make it in to pick them up."

Mary's shoulders drooped.

"Tom Svezic?" she asked.

"Yes, Tom Svezic."

"Couldn't I drop it off at his sister's house?" Mary asked. "It's just down the street."

Cynthia gave Mary a questioning look.

"I know where she lives," Cynthia replied. "But Tom's sister doesn't work at the mine. I realize it's a long walk, and you're tired, but he'll need those clothes when he goes back to work." Cynthia paused. She closed her eyes and took a slow, deep breath. "And I don't want you taking any short cuts. You have enough scrapes and bruises as it is."

"I know, Mom. Don't run, stay on the sidewalks, and go straight there and come straight back. And don't talk to strangers."

"And don't forget to collect the money," Cynthia reminded her. "He owes me two dollars and fifteen cents for last month." Cynthia walked over to Mary and helped her with her boots and coat. "And don't put the money in the pocket with the hole. I haven't had time to mend it."

"I won't, Mom."

Cynthia fastened the last button on Mary's coat, smiled as she caressed the Silver Star, and then walked over to a chair to enjoy a few minutes of rest before preparing supper.

Mary walked over and stroked her mother's hair.

"It's going to be all right, Mom. I know it will."

Cynthia gave her a kiss and a hug.

"I believe you," she said. "Now, you better go before it gets too late."

Mary skipped down the sidewalk, humming "Hark the Herald Angels Sing" and paying little attention to anything except the decorated storefront windows. Every once in a while she would stop to look at everything she couldn't have. After admiring a certain dress, she turned and bumped into someone on the sidewalk.

"Watch out!" the man yelled.

Mary dropped the bundle of clothes.

Blocking her way were two drunks who had just left the saloon--the Turpin brothers, a couple the town's more prominent near-do-wells. Mary knew the family well from her personal contact with them and from the rumors and gossip she heard. She didn't believe half the stories, but the half she did believe was bad enough.

≈≈

Billy Turpin was twenty-two-years-old. He had dark hair that was slicked down with oil and combed straight back. He had small beady eyes, a weak chin, and was as thin as a rail. The scent of his clothes irritated the nose, and his hands were coated with grease. He was constantly getting into trouble and was always getting caught.

His brother Jimmy was four inches taller, fifty pounds heavier and two years older but mentally ten years his junior. He had short-cropped hair, stubby whiskers, and several chipped teeth in the front of his mouth. He wore coveralls and shirts that hadn't felt the affects of soap and water since his last dunk in the creek--his solution to the summer heat while satisfying the needs of cleanliness and hygiene.

Their father, *Daddy*, while alive, believed in the liberal use of the razor strap on the backs of his disobedient children. Everyone in town feared him. He was an alcoholic, a troublemaker, and was always on the prowl for an easy dollar and a good time.

The boys' mother left home when Billy turned eighteen, while she was still able to duck Daddy's drunken punches. She was never seen or heard from again. Some of the townspeople said she blamed herself for not being able to change Daddy's evil ways or raise the boys in a Christian manner. Others feared Daddy might have done her in when he was in one of his fits of rage, but nothing ever came of Sheriff Durben's investigation, or so he claimed, and the subject was dropped from polite conversation.

"Excuse me, Mr. *Turdpin*," Mary said, stepping aside.

"The name is Turpin. Mr. Billy Turpin to you, brat."

Jimmy stepped forward and belched. "Yeah, Mr. Turpin."

Billy circled Mary. He looked her over as if she was Little Red Riding Hood, and he was the Big Bad Wolf. He picked something out of his teeth with his fingernail and smiled as if a thought had suddenly found its way into his alcohol-soaked brain.

Jimmy leaned against a nearby storefront wall to maintain his balance.

Billy smiled and asked Mary all too sweetly, "Aren't you Cynthia Klein's darling little daughter?"

He picked up the bundle of clothes and handed it to her. Mary nodded yes. Her hands shook. She took the bundle and moved back.

"If you'll excuse me, Mr. Turpin," Mary said, "I have to take these clothes to Tom Svezic's place."

"That's a long walk from here," Billy noted. "You better be careful," he said, looking into Mary's eyes. "We wouldn't want anything to happen to you along the way. Would we?" he said, turning to his brother.

Jimmy covered his mouth with his hand and laughed.

"I better go," Mary said. "My mom will worry if I'm late."

"Then, leave!" Billy yelled.

He waved his hands in the air like a spook on Halloween, and Mary ran away, full speed.

# Chapter XII

Cynthia was at the kitchen sink cleaning the last of the potatoes and green beans for supper when the front door squeaked open. The cold air from the street drifted across the floor and brushed her feet. A shiver ran down her spine.

"Did you forget something, Honey?" she asked.

"No, Honey," Billy answered with a snicker. Cynthia turned, and Billy stepped inside. Jimmy followed, stumbling into him. "Watch the door," Billy said, shoving Jimmy away. Jimmy closed the door and leaned against it. Billy grabbed his brother's arm and shook him. "I mean, watch from the outside, you idiot."

"But..." Jimmy stammered.

"I can do this alone," Billy replied, opening the door.

Jimmy seemed confused and alarmed, but he did as he was told. When he was gone, Billy closed the door.

"You better get out of here," Cynthia said. "Before you get into real trouble."

"Not until I get the money," Billy answered.

He took a step forward and then another; his gate was slow and shaky. Cynthia slipped her hand into the sink. Her eyes narrowed, and her anger grew. When he reached out to grab her, she threw a handful of green beans into his face, pushed him aside, and ran for the front door.

"No you don't," Billy said, stumbling after her.

He caught her cotton work dress and pulled her back. She fought to get away, but he wrapped his arm around her neck. She couldn't breathe; struggling was futile, so she stopped.

"That's more like it," Billy said. He loosened his grip and pulled her over to a chair. "Sit here, and don't yell. No one will hear you anyway." His body swayed from side to side like a reed against the tide. "I know you know where the bank money is, at least Sylvester's share," he said, pointing his finger at her. "So tell me where it's at, and I'll leave you alone." Cynthia crossed her arms and stared at him in silence. "Where is it?" he yelled. Cynthia looked away. "Is it here in the house?" Billy's patience ended as he waited for a reply and saw none forthcoming. "Then, I guess I'll have to find it myself."

He rummaged through the house like a blind man searching for sunlight in the middle of the night. He knocked over chairs, fought with the wash hanging on the lines, fell against the furniture, and pushed aside whatever was in his way. The more he looked for the money, the angrier he became and the more damage he did. But when he entered the bedroom and Mary's music box played, Cynthia jumped to her feet as the little ballerina danced to the tune of "Let Me Call You Sweetheart."

"No!" she yelled. "Don't you dare touch that!"

She ran over to Billy, kicked him in the shins, and took the music box out of his hands before he knew what had happened.

"Why don't you leave us alone?" she said. "We don't have the money."

She put the music box on the kitchen table, grabbed a chair, and held it in front of her like a lion tamer facing a beast. Whenever Billy came forward, she pushed him back. It looked more like a dance than a struggle; though Billy hardly had the lead, and he tripped constantly over his own two feet.

"Where is it?" Billy growled. "He had to tell someone, and there's only you and the kid."

He reached out for her and stumbled into the chair, but she shoved him away, and he fell against one of the wringer washers.

"Get out of here, you drunken pig!" she yelled.

"Pig!" Billy shouted. He slapped the water in the tub and ran toward her, "I'll show you."

Before she could react, he wrestled the chair out of her hands and threw it against the wall.

"Where's it at?" he hollered.

Cynthia's face flared red. She raised her arms and yelled, "It's not here!"

The front door swung open; wind raced through the house. The clothes on the line shuddered, and the little Christmas tree shook to the rhythm of the ringing of a tiny silver bell.

Jimmy bounced into the room like a rubber ball and rolled to a stop at his brother's feet. Cynthia retreated behind the kitchen table.

"Rosey," Billy said with a gulp.

Rosey walked over to Billy and lifted him by the throat. Billy couldn't breathe; he couldn't speak. He danced on his tiptoes like the music box ballerina.

"I ought to tear you limb from limb," Rosey snarled.

Billy pulled at Rosey's arm, but as hard as he tried, he couldn't set himself free. Billy's face turned red, his eyes bulged, and his tongue dangled from his mouth.

Jimmy whimpered and crawled to the door.

Rosey turned to Jimmy. "Where do you think you're going?"

Cynthia cried out, "No, Rosey. Don't hurt them."

Tears poured from her eyes.

Rosey's muscles trembled; the silver bell chimed, and Billy fell to the floor, coughing and holding his neck.

Rosey took a deep breath and walked over to Cynthia.

"Did he hurt you?" Rosey asked.

Cynthia shook her head no.

Rosey walked over to Billy and looked around the room. Billy cringed.

Rosey pointed his finger at him and said, "I think you owe the lady an apology, and some money for wrecking her house."

"We're sorry," Billy said, stuttering.

He trembled from head to toe. It was all he could do to stand. He reached into his pocket and pulled out a couple of one-dollar bills, two dimes, a nickel, and a shriveled something he had found on side of the road.

"Get out of here!" Rosey yelled.

Billy dropped his cache and was out the door before the money hit the floor.

Cynthia walked around the house, straightening things as she went along.

Her voice quivered. "I can't let Mary see this mess. She's been through enough as it is."

"Where is she?" Rosey asked.

"She took some clothes over to Tom Svezic."

Cynthia picked a safety pin off the floor and pinned her torn dress.

Rosey placed his hand on her arm. "I'll go get her." He took a handkerchief out of his pocket and handed it to Cynthia. "Will you be all right here alone?"

"I'll be fine," she said, drying her eyes.

"I don't know," Rosey replied, hesitantly. "Maybe I should give Doc a call. You could be hurt and not even know it."

"No. Don't do that. Please," Cynthia implored. "I'm all right."

"If that's the way you want it," Rosey said.

"It's the way it has to be, believe me."

"At least promise me you'll go lie down."

"I will after I clean up this mess."

"And don't you worry about Mary," Rosey said. "I'll take her to Flo's for supper. And I'll bring you back something to eat."

"It's really not necessary."

Rosey took her hand and silenced her with his touch.

"To what, help a friend?" Rosey looked around the room, paused, and then scratched his neck. "What did the Turpins want?"

"The money," Cynthia said. "They all want the money."

"Do you want to press charges?" Rosey asked.

"No. I can't do that. I just want to be left alone."

"I understand, but I'm going to have to tell Sheriff Durben. He has to know." Cynthia started to speak, and Rosey raised his hand to silence her. "I promise you there won't be any trouble. I'll take care of everything."

"Thank you, Rosey. You were always a good friend to Sylvester and me."

"Sylvester is still my friend," Rosey said firmly. "And when he's finally cleared of the charges and set free, I'll see that he gets his job back as our billing agent. Now, I want you to rest until I bring Mary home. I'll tell her you're not feeling good."

# Chapter XIII

Tom Svezic lived in a vacant feed store. Over the years he had made several renovations to include the application of numerous coats of varnish to the wood floors and paint to the walls, but despite his best efforts, the odor of wheat, corn, and fertilizer still permeated the building. Mary believed that the lingering odor of the varnish, combined with the resident aromas, somehow contributed to Tom's illness. In any case, the smell made Mary's nose tickle, which in turn made her sneeze for several minutes after her visits. When Rosey arrived, she was at the front door, blowing her nose in the handkerchief Paul had given her.

"There you are," Rosey said with a bigger than usual smile. He paused before approaching. "I have a surprise for you."

"A surprise, for me?" Mary asked, sneezing.

"Bless you," Rosey said.

"Thank you," Mary replied, blowing her nose. "What is it?"

Mary put the handkerchief in her coat pocket.

Rosey smiled and tilted his head to one side.

"How would you like a meal befitting a royal princess?" Rosey bowed to her in an awkward manner and said, "To be exact, supper with me at the best diner in Mayfield."

He took a step forward and reached with outstretched arms in an attempt to liberate her feet from the earth, but Mary moved away. She felt one of his hugs before when he came over to get his clean work clothes. She didn't mind the squeeze, even though it was a bit too hard and much too long, but her body dangling in the air was unsettling. He also had a bad habit of hugging, walking, and squeezing while holding her and carrying on a conversation, all at the same time. A combination she found somewhat traumatic.

"I don't know," Mary replied. "It's getting late, and Mom might worry if I don't come right back."

"It's all right. I just left her. She's a bit under the weather, but it's nothing for you to worry about. I think she's just been working too hard and needs a little rest." Rosey put his hand on Mary's head. "Believe it or not, even I myself sometimes get tired on occasion and need to sit down and relax." Rosey took Mary's hand, and they walked down the sidewalk to the diner. "Tonight, I decided to take the prettiest girl in town out to supper. You might say it's one of my Christmas presents."

"A Christmas present for me?" Mary asked.

"Actually, it's more of a Christmas present for me," Rosey said with a chuckle.

When they reached the diner, they stopped to look through the picture window. The window had the words *Flo's Diner* painted on it in large, white letters.

Mary tugged Rosey's hand, and he bent down.

Mary whispered, "You know, them people inside sure eat a lot."

Rosey grinned. "They work hard, and when you work hard you eat hardy."

"Me and Mom work hard, but we've never been in there. It's too ritzy, Mom says, but I stop sometimes and look inside. Once, when someone opened the door, I stuck my head in and smelled the food. It didn't smell ritzy to me."

Rosey let out a short laugh and opened the door.

"After you, me lady."

Mary tilted her head up to look at Rosey.

"Are you sure you can afford this?" Mary asked. "It's a funny Christmas present if you ask me."

"I most assuredly can afford it, but I may not deserve it," Rosey said. There was sadness in his reply. "Let's sit by the window so we can look at the people outside and pretend we're the royal court out on the town."

Rosey took Mary by the hand and escorted her to a table. He gallantly pulled the chair out for her with an outstretched arm in a show of good spirit, and then sat in the chair across from her.

"I see you have a date tonight," Florence said in her other role as waitress.

"You might say that, Flo. However, I think the princess is much too beautiful and charming for someone like me."

"No I'm not!" Mary said forcefully.

Rosey shook his head and said, "Why, thank you, little princess."

Flo leaned forward and said to Rosey as if repeating a secret intended for their table only, "I hear the mine will be working a lot of overtime in the coming months."

"You can say that again," Rosey replied. "The boys are only going to have time to eat, sleep and..." Mary leaned forward and Rosey paused. "We better order," he said.

Rosey's face was flushed. Flo quietly laughed and took a pencil and pad out of her apron pocket.

"What can I bring you and the princess?" Flo asked with a slight curtsy and a subdued smile.

Rosey looked at the chalkboard on the wall and said, "I'll have tonight's meatloaf special with peas, potatoes, and a large mug of root beer to wash it down."

Flo turned to Mary and asked, "And what will the princess have?"

Rosey tapped Flo on the arm and said with a nod to Mary, "I'll order for the princess from the menu." Flo handed Rosey a menu and waited while he studied it. "Let's see. How about a thick, juicy steak?"

"No," Mary answered, shaking her head.

"How about some chicken and dumplings?"

"No," she replied again.

"Hmm, I know," Rosey said. "How about a chocolate ice cream sundae with a big red cherry on top?"

Mary's eyes grew to twice their size.

"I thought so," Rosey said, fingering down the menu. "But first I think you will have a plate of spaghetti with meat balls and lots of sauce."

Mary smiled and said, "I love spaghetti and meatballs. They're my favorite."

"Then spaghetti it is, followed by a chocolate ice cream sundae with a big, red cherry on top."

Rosey winked at Mary and handed Flo the menu.

"Will that be all?" Flo asked.

"Not quite," Rosey said. He motioned for Flo to come nearer. "I'd like one special to take with me. I'll bring the plate back tomorrow, if that's all right?"

"Of course, but you better watch that spread," Flo said, poking his stomach with her pencil.

"It's not for me," Rosey quickly answered.

"Of course not," Flo said, leaving.

There was a moment of silence as Rosey studied the bulge under his shirt. Mary smiled in a slow and deliberate manner. It was as if she took more delight in the process than in the finished product. It began with a grin and a slight tilt of the head that was followed by a twinkle in her eyes. Rosey appeared nervous. He watched her changing expression and tapped his fingers on the table. Mary looked around the diner to see if anyone was within listening distance, then bent over the table and signaled with the bending of her index finger for Rosey to come closer so no one passing by would hear what she had to say.

"Do you think the bank robber could still be hiding in Mayfield somewhere?" she asked.

Rosey pulled back and scratched his head. The question seemed to have taken him by surprise.

"I think it's possible," he answered. "But not likely. It would be hard for the robber to remain incognito with all that money burning a hole in his pocket."

"Incognito?" Mary asked.

"Anonymous," Rosey answered.

Mary frowned. Rosey searched for an easier explanation.

"It's like seeing a crowd of people with everyone wearing a red shirt. They all look the same so no one looks unusual. But if one of them wore a yellow shirt, he would be easy to spot, now wouldn't he?"

"I guess he would," Mary replied. "Do you think the robber could have done this before, somewhere else?"

"That's possible," Rosey said. "It's not uncommon for a bank robber to keep robbing banks, until he's caught, anyway." Rosey leaned forward and squinted. "Why all the questions?"

Mary looked at the ceiling and ignored his stare, but Rosey persisted. Mary placed her hand under the table and crossed her fingers.

"I was just talking to someone I met," she said, "and the subject came up. That's all."

"Do I know this someone you met?" Rosey asked.

"I don't think so. He's no one, really," Mary replied.

Mary evaded Rosey's piercing eyes and searched the diner for a friendly face. She focused on Flo, who was removing some dirty dishes from a nearby table. Flo waved and Mary smiled. Rosey's stare remained fixed, and Mary's resolve melted away.

"We only talked," she said.

"Go on. What else?" Rosey asked.

"You mustn't tell anyone. Promise?"

"I'll keep my promise if I can," he replied.

Mary took a breath before answering.

"His name is Angelo. I met him in the woods by the railroad trestle. I fell down at the sledding hill, and he bandaged my hand."

Rosey was surprised by her answer. It took him a moment to reply.

"I was wondering what happened to your hand," he said. "This Angelo fellow, is he why you're asking these questions?"

Rosey's tone of voice changed from that of a friend to that of an interrogator.

Mary looked away and said, "Here comes Flo."

Rosey stared at Mary as Flo put the plates and drinks on the table, but Mary ignored him.

"Here you are, Princess," Flo said. "Enjoy your meal." Flo turned to Rosey. "I'll have your take-out waiting for you at the cash register when you leave."

Rosey nodded, then lowered his head in prayer. Mary echoed his Amen, and then strand by strand she inhaled the spaghetti. After all the pasta was eaten, and the last meatball devoured, she attacked the chocolate ice cream sundae with the big red cherry on top.

Rosey signaled Flo. A minute later she came to the table with the bill in one hand and a damp face cloth in the other. Mary flinched in anticipation of an after-dinner mopping, but Flo just smiled and handed her the face cloth.

The dinner eaten and the bill paid, Mary and Rosey followed their full bellies out the door. Rosey escorted his Princess home, hand-in-hand, down the snow-carpeted sidewalks, receiving a tender kiss from two gentle spirits at the end of the journey for a funny Christmas present and a plate of the special.

# Chapter XIV

J effrey stood in front of his office window and stared out into the street. He saw everything, yet recognized nothing. He didn't want to stay, but he didn't know where to go. He hadn't eaten all day, and his stomach had long since given up reminding him of the fact.

Someone knocked on the front door. Jeffrey shook the cobwebs out of his head and left his office to see who it was. He pulled back the window shade and was greeted by Paul's smiling face. He would have preferred to return the shade to its original position, and he to his, but he opened the door instead.

"What in heaven's name are you still doing here?" Paul asked.

"Working, of course," Jeffrey answered. "What else would I be doing here?"

Jeffrey turned and went back to his office. Paul closed the door and followed.

"What do you mean, working?" Paul asked.

"I mean working." Jeffrey said. His hands were animated; his face was full of expression. "There are accounts to be updated, investments to be made, money to be transferred, ledgers to check...things to do."

"Things, my foot," Paul replied. "You're still trying to pay everyone back from the robbery, aren't you?"

Jeffrey didn't answer. He paced the office, and then walked over to the window. Paul came over and stood by his side. They looked out at Main Street with its decorated storefronts, wreath-covered lampposts, and package-laden shoppers. It was a cheerful scene, but one alien to the confines of the office.

A group of people smiled and waved as they passed the window. Paul waved back. Jeffrey nodded coldly in reply.

"Look out there," Jeffrey said. "You wouldn't believe anything bad could happen here, especially at this time of year."

"It can happen anywhere, anytime," Paul answered. "No one can escape the tragedies of this world or predict when they're going to happen, or wish them away when they do. I told you before, and I'm telling you again, it's time you quit torturing yourself and let the past go before it ruins your life."

Jeffrey turned his back to the window, walked over to his chair, and sat.

"Why are you here?" he asked. "Did Marge call you?"

"No, Marge didn't call me," Paul answered. "I was returning from the Toller place, when I saw you standing in front of the window. I remembered you were supposed to take the statue over to the church this afternoon." Paul looked at his watch. "And you're late. Did you forget?"

Jeffrey shut his eyes and said, "Good God, I was, wasn't I?"

"You've forgotten a lot of things lately," Paul reminded him, "but we don't have time to discuss that now. If we hurry, we can get the statue and make it to church before everyone leaves." Paul walked over to the office door. "I'll drive. You sit and think about what I said."

When they arrived at the church, the steeple bells were tolling the hour. The choir was singing a Christmas carol, "The First Noel," Paul's favorite. Paul listened and hummed along, while Jeffrey got the statue out of the car's trunk.

"Let's go," Jeffrey said.

Paul faced the church. "Look at that," he said.

"Look at what," Jeffrey answered.

"At that," Paul said, pointing. "It's like a painting, except with music."

Jeffrey shook his head and said, "Let's get this over with. This crate is getting heavy."

Paul and Jeffrey entered the vestibule. Jeffrey stepped into the doorway and was about to make his appearance when Paul pulled him back.

"Wait a minute," Paul whispered. "I feel like Daniel standing in front of the lion's den. Let's see what's going on in there first."

Jeffrey peeked around the corner. Paul was by his side.

The choir director called the end of rehearsal in a voice that rumbled throughout the church like a boulder, and then led the choir down from the loft. The tramping of the footsteps brought goose pumps to Jeffrey's arms.

"Well," the choir director huffed. She placed her hands on her hips and faced the assembled mass of parishioners. "I told you he wouldn't show up with the statue."

Another woman spoke out, "I was hoping to see the statue after choir practice, but I guess that was too much to ask?"

Reverend Richmann was in the pulpit, as was his normal practice, reviewing Sunday's sermon. When he heard the complaints, he put away his notes and spoke in a calm voice. "Jeffrey said he'd be here, and he'll be here. Something must have happened. We'll give him ten more minutes, and then I'll give him a call."

The choir director walked to the altar. Her voice was sharp. "I say we go to his house and get the statue."

Her words took everyone by surprise. When the shock wore off, the discussion began.

"Please settle down," one of the men said. His wife nudged him in the side, but he shrugged it off and continued. "Jeffrey knows he's supposed to be here. Let's give him ten more minutes like Reverend Richmann said."

"Ten more minutes and I leave," one of the choir members said. "We've waited long enough, and I'm getting hungry."

The pastor raised his arms to quell the emotional outflow, and to say something on Jeffrey's behalf, but he only got a few words out when Paul gave Jeffrey a shove and they entered. Jeffrey held the crate as if it were filled with eggs.

"Here he is, safe and sound," the reverend said.

Jeffrey smiled and said in response as he walked down the aisle, head held high and shoulders back. "I apologize for my tardiness. I was working late at the office and completely lost track of the time."

"I knew you'd be here," Pastor Richmann said with a sigh of relief. "Bring the statue to the altar so we may all see it."

Jeffrey stopped at the altar steps, put the crate on the floor, and carefully pried off the top with his pocket knife. As soon as the crate was opened, everyone gathered around to see the statue. Jeffrey was unceremoniously pushed to the rear of the crowd.

"He's marvelous," the choir director said, touching the statue's hand.

The pastor picked up the statue and cradled it in his arms like a newborn.

"The white marble looks as pure as fresh fallen snow," Pastor Richmann said. He caressed the statue's face and smiled. "But warm with the gentle radiance of love."

"I say we put the statue over here for tomorrow's church service," one of the parishioners said.

She scooted the crate along the floor to its proposed resting place.

"Yeah, directly in front of the pew you sit in," someone said in a muffled voice.

"I think it should be placed closer to the pulpit," Jeffrey suggested.

"Of course you would," the choir director said. She pointed to a large brass plate on the front of the pulpit stating that Jeffrey's father had donated it. "If you had your way, you'd brand the statue with the Carston crest."

Paul stepped forward and said, "No need to get nasty. Jeffrey put a lot of time and effort into getting this statue."

"That doesn't give him any more rights than the rest of us," the choir director replied.

"That will be enough!" Pastor Richmann cried out. "They'll be no more bickering over the statue." Pastor Richmann's face was red. Everyone paused as he returned the statue to the crate and walked over to the pulpit. "All our parishioners attending church service Sunday must receive a benefit from the position of the manger. Therefore, the statue will be placed inside the vestibule by the front doors. That way everyone will be able to see the statue when they enter and leave the church. As for taking the statue to the grotto on Christmas Eve, I was hoping Jeffrey would be kind enough to stop by the church sometime in the afternoon and take care of that little chore for us."

"Excellent idea," Paul said.

The women groaned their displeasure, but Pastor Richmann ignored them.

"Then, it's settled," the pastor said. "Tonight, we'll leave the statue where it is. Tomorrow, I'll get one of the folding tables out of the rectory's basement and place it in the vestibule." Pastor Richmann's stomach growled. He coughed to muffle the rumble. "You may all stay here to look at the statue as long as you wish, but I have to go to the rectory to finish my sermon and get something to eat. It's been a long day," he said with a sigh. "I'll come back later to take care of the statue and to turn out the lights."

The pastor walked down the aisle, his head fixed, looking neither right nor left as he made his way to the exit. Paul looked at the swarm of women milling around the altar, tapped Jeffrey on the arm, and asked him if he were ready to go. Jeffrey hesitated, and then nodded yes.

Once outside, Paul smiled in recognition of their escape. He was still smiling when he noticed Sheriff Durben waiting for him in the parking lot. Paul's smile, however, drooped when he observed the sheriff's foot resting on the rear bumper of his car.

"Hello, Sheriff," Paul said in an irritated tone. "Come for a little religion or to scrape the bottoms of your shoes off on my car's bumper?"

"Neither," Sheriff Durben replied. "I came for you."

The sheriff was clearly distraught. He removed his foot from the bumper and walked over to the passenger side of the car. Paul and Jeffrey followed.

"What did Paul do now?" Jeffrey asked. "Fill another inside straight?"

"This is no joking matter," the sheriff replied.

"What's wrong?" Paul asked.

Sheriff Durben took the cigar stub out of his mouth and examined it for life. It was beyond revival.

"The Turpin brothers broke into Cynthia Klein's house earlier this evening."

"No," Jeffrey said.

He stepped to the side and looked at the stars. He felt no emotions, and it scared him.

"Was anyone injured?" Paul asked.

"I don't think so. Luckily, Rosey happened to stop by for his work clothes while the Turpins were there. Mary was out running an errand." The sheriff threw his cigar away and spat a bit of tobacco into the snow. "Cynthia doesn't want to press charges. I guess she's afraid."

"Of course she's afraid," Paul answered. "Why wouldn't she be afraid? She certainly has good cause."

The sheriff peeled the cellophane wrapper off a fresh cigar and put the cigar into his mouth.

"Would you stop by and check on her just to make sure that she's all right?" the sheriff asked.

"Of course, but why did they break in?" Paul asked.

"Rosey said they were after the bank money."

Jeffrey stepped closer.

Paul crossed his arms and said, "Surely those two boys aren't stupid enough to think that Cynthia has the money from the robbery." Paul took a deep breath. "Oh well, I suppose most of the town fits into that category. Maybe she has it stashed away in a cookie jar, if she has a cookie jar, or perhaps she has it stowed away under her bed with the rest of her treasure."

Paul huffed and took a step back.

"What are you going to do?" Jeffrey asked Sheriff Durben.

Sheriff Durben took the cigar out of his mouth, rolled it between his fingers as he examined it, and then placed it back into his mouth.

"As far as I'm concerned," he replied, the cigar firmly secured between his teeth, "those two boys have worn out their welcome in this town. Ever since Daddy died they've taken over his share of the gas station and mischief as well."

Sheriff Durben took a match out of his pocket and struck it against his belt buckle. The match tip broke off and the sheriff grumbled.

"Given the way their father raised them," Paul said, "you could hardly expect them to be model citizens. Cents for sense, those boys wouldn't have enough between them to buy a candy bar."

"Daddy Turpin was plenty mean," Jeffrey said. "We crossed paths on more than one occasion; it wasn't pleasant." Jeffrey took a breath. "He followed me around for days after the robbery. When I confronted him, he claimed I was in on it. He said he wanted his share or he'd tell the sheriff." Jeffrey gave Sheriff Durben a nod and continued. "The man was crazy. After that, he had his boys follow me. If Daddy hadn't died from that stroke, I dare say those boys would still be following me. I kind of feel sorry for them."

"And the Kleins?" Paul asked with an aggravated tone.

He stared at Jeffrey. Jeffrey looked back, but said nothing.

Sheriff Durben retrieved another match from his pocket and lit his cigar. He took a long drag, raised his head, and blew the smoke skyward.

"I think it's time to go over to Turpin's filling station and throw a little scare into those two boys." Sheriff Durben walked toward his patrol car, but stopped after a few steps. "By the way," he said, turning, "have either of you seen any strangers hanging around town lately?"

"Strangers? Why no," Jeffrey answered.

"Why?" Paul asked.

"Nothing important," Sheriff Durben said. "Just something Rosey told me."

The sheriff waved good-bye with a flick of the wrist, and then walked away, leaving a trail of smoke.

"What do you think?" Jeffrey asked Paul.

"About what, the Sheriff's smoking?"

"No, about the Turpin boys?"

"Two words come to mind: imbeciles and morons.

# Chapter XV

The light from Sheriff Durben's patrol car streaked through the front window of the Turpin brothers' house. When the sheriff got out of the car, he saw the figure of a man in the window and heard the radio playing. As he walked to the house, someone pulled the blinds down.

Sheriff Durben pounded on the front door with his fist.

"Open up!" he shouted. The radio went silent. "Let me in, you idiots. I know you're in there."

He kicked the doorframe and smudged his freshly polished boots. Angrier, he yelled all the louder for them to open the door.

"I'm coming," a muffled voice said.

Sheriff Durben stepped back. He heard the slow pace of footsteps. The door cracked open just wide enough for a nose to be seen, Billy's nose. Sheriff Durben blew a cloud of smoke into the protruding orifice, and Billy coughed.

The sheriff pushed his way in. Billy caught his breath and blamed Cynthia for everything that had happened before the sheriff could say a word. Sheriff Durben, however, wasn't in the mood for lies or other prattle from the likes of the Turpins. He stared into Billy's eyes and backed him against the pantry. Billy's courage flowed from his body in a cold sweat.

Sheriff Durben poked his finger into Billy's chest.

"Stay here and don't move," the sheriff ordered.

He walked over to Jimmy, but kept looking back at Billy who was, by now, as pale as a ghost. Jimmy sat by the radio in a rickety old chair that creaked as his body shook. He held a peanut butter jar in one hand and a spoon in the other. His mouth was full of Peter Pan's best. Saliva squirted from his lips and oozed down his chin.

"Swallow!" Sheriff Durben ordered. He waited for Jimmy to clear his throat. It took several tries. "Tell me why you went to Cynthia Klein's house."

Jimmy wiped his mouth with his shirtsleeve and spoke. The words stuck like glue in his peanut butter coated mouth. "Billy wanted to get the stolen bank money."

Jimmy pointed his spoon at Billy. Some peanut butter fell to the floor. Sheriff Durben moved his shoe out of the way.

"What else?" the sheriff asked.

Jimmy trembled, the chair squeaked. "Nothing," Jimmy replied. "We didn't want no trouble, just the bank money." He licked the spoon clean and put it into the jar. "Rosey came soon after we got there, and we left."

The sheriff put his hand on Jimmy's shoulder and gave him a firm but sympathetic pat. His voice was calm.

"Why did you think Mrs. Klein had the money?" the sheriff asked.

Jimmy gulped.

"Daddy said Sylvester took it from the bank and hid it. Billy knows. Daddy always told Billy things, not me."

Billy shook his head in denial and said, "He doesn't know what he is talking about."

Billy took a step forward in protest. When he realized what he had done, he moved back. The sheriff patted Jimmy on the shoulder in a somewhat comforting manner and walked over to Billy.

"What made Daddy think Sylvester had the money?" Sheriff Durben asked. "Sylvester claimed he didn't take it."

Billy looked away and said, "Everybody knows Sylvester lied. Daddy said so."

The sheriff puffed his cigar. A cloud of smoke cloaked Billy's head.

"What else did Daddy say?"

Billy coughed and fanned the smoke away.

"Daddy said a lot of things. He was always talking about the money, but that's all. It was only talk. You know how Daddy was."

"Following Mr. Carston was more than talk," Sheriff Durben said. "Why did Daddy have you follow him?"

Billy looked at Jimmy, and then spoke. "Daddy said rich folks always want more. He figured since no one is spending the money, someone is hiding it, maybe Mr. Carston or Mrs. Klein, maybe even one of the children.

"One of the children!" Sheriff Durben yelled. "What about the children?"

Billy's eyes widened. He raised his hands and said, "Nothing, honest. Daddy sometimes said things he didn't mean, especially when he had too much to drink. It was just the bottle talking. The next day he'd forget what he said, like it never happened."

"That's one thing you better forget," Sheriff Durben replied. He pointed his cigar at Billy. "And while we're on the subject, I don't like what you did to Mrs. Klein. People who do those sorts of things shouldn't be allowed on the streets with decent folks."

The sheriff slid his hand to his holster and unfastened the safety strap with his thumb. The metal snap emitted a loud click against the revolver.

Billy fell to the floor and covered his head with his hands.

"Don't Sheriff. We won't do nothing. We promise."

The sheriff bent down and spoke into the top of Billy's head. "You're a liar, and a troublemaker."

The sheriff walked to the center of the room and stood, eyeing Billy like a snake a rat. He wanted to grab Billy by the neck and shake the devil out of him. Jimmy clicked his spoon against the peanut butter jar. The sheriff turned. Jimmy froze.

The sheriff slapped his holster.

"If either of you come within a hundred feet of Mrs. Klein or her daughter, I'll arrest you and blow your brains out, if I can hit anything that small. Do you understand?"

"Yeah, yeah, we understand," the brothers whimpered.

Jimmy rolled himself into a ball. Billy sat on the floor and hugged his legs.

Sheriff Durben walked to the door. His muscles twitched, and his heart pounded.

"Nitwits," he said, turning around. "You're just lucky there isn't a law against stupidity."

Sheriff Durben slammed the door shut and took a couple of long drags on his cigar to calm himself down. He could hear the Turpins inside arguing over who had said what. But there was nothing more he could do, so he went back to his patrol car and drove full speed out of town toward a secluded bar and grill where the people didn't ask questions, and the food was complimentary for him and his deputies.

# Chapter XVI

A ngelo was on the road by the grotto, singing as he walked, his tote sack draped over his shoulder, and a small dog attached by the teeth to his coattail.

"Hark the herald angels sing...Quit it!" Angelo said. A light appeared on the road in the distance. "Here comes another one." Angelo shook the dog off and ran behind a tree. But the dog, to Angelo's dismay, jumped, twisted, and then reattached himself to Angelo's coattail as an old flatbed truck drove by. "This is sure a busy road tonight, and you aren't making the going any easier." Angelo pointed his finger at the dog. "Lucky for you no one ever pays attention to people like me or animals like you." The dog whined in reply. Angelo paused to give his words some thought. "Perhaps they're afraid we'll ask them for a handout." The dog barked and stood on his hind legs, begging. Angelo grinned and reached into his tote sack. "You're fortunate I'm not one of them. How about a ham bone?" The dog barked and danced in a circle. "I'm afraid it doesn't have much meat on it," he said, dangling the bone in the air, "but it should have enough to satisfy a creature your size."

Angelo tossed the bone on the road. The dog ran after the scrap of food, and then sat contentedly gnawing and chewing. Angelo tiptoed away and limped up the mountain path to observe the stars and think.

The sky was clear, but a light mist hovered around him like an oyster's shell. He loved the mountain. It was the closest place to heaven, and it made him feel at ease, but tonight he sensed danger. He wondered if he would ever see home again.

He heard the sound of a car's horn, and the sliding of wheels on the slick pavement. Just another driver in a hurry to get somewhere else, he thought. It was a common enough occurrence, especially on this part of the road. Then, he remembered the dog and went over to the edge of the cliff to see if the dog was all right.

"Don't move!" Sheriff Durben said in a commanding voice. He stood at the bottom of the path, threw his cigar away, and rubbed a handful of snow on his pants leg. "Another pair ruined," he said angrily." Angelo took a step back, and Sheriff Durben yelled, "I said don't move! I'm the sheriff. Is your name Angelo?"

Angelo didn't answer. Sheriff Durben asked again, but Angelo couldn't speak. He feared it was the end, and there was nothing he could do.

"Stay where you're at," Sheriff Durben ordered. "I'm coming up."

The sheriff was halfway there when something jumped out from a bush and grabbed his leg.

"Get off me!" Sheriff Durben shouted. "The next time I'm running you over."

The little dog had attached itself by the teeth to the sheriff's pants and apparently wanted to stay attached. The sheriff had other ideas.

"Beat it, you mutt!" Sheriff Durben yelled.

He swung at the dog, but the dog let go, and the sheriff slipped--tumbling, bouncing, and yelling as he fell. Angelo was shocked by the sudden turn in events. He wanted to help, but all he could do was watch.

When the deed was done, Angelo went down. The sheriff lay motionless on his back in the snow. The dog sat by the sheriff's head. He licked the sheriff's face and whimpered his apology. Angelo knelt next to the sheriff and examined him for broken bones. The sheriff moaned and moved his arms and legs. He opened his eyes, but he couldn't focus. When the examination was done, Angelo let out a sigh of relief, reached into his tote sack, pulled out an old, broad rimmed hat, and placed it under the sheriff's head.

The dog growled.

"Quiet," Angelo said. "I don't care if you did find it in the cave. It doesn't belong to you, and he needs it. Besides, it's the least you can do after what you did to him." Angelo pushed the dog away and spoke to the sheriff. "You're going to be fine. Nothing seems to be broken, and there's no sign of blood, but you do have a nasty bump on the back of your head." Sheriff Durben rolled his eyes and mumbled something about kings and queens and wedding rings.

Angelo looked scornfully at the dog, shook his finger and said, "Bad dog. I thought I taught you better than that." The dog lowered his head and walked away, his tail between his legs. Angelo looked at the sheriff. "He didn't mean to make you fall, but sometimes the puppy in him gets out of control." Angelo stood and brushed the snow off his clothes. "I'm truly sorry, but I can't stay here with you. I have things to do, and I don't think you'd let me go in your present state of mind."

Angelo limped down the road, scolding the little dog along the way.

❦

The sheriff sat up and saw a man and a dog walking away. Actually, two men and two dogs, both dogs were wagging their tails. A few minutes later, the sheriff went back to his patrol car and radioed for assistance. When the deputy arrived, he wanted to take Sheriff Durben to the county hospital, but the sheriff wasn't about to be treated by any state-trained professional. It was only a bump on the head. Paul was doctor enough to handle a bump. It didn't matter that Paul usually went to bed early. The sheriff believed that anyone who could fill an inside straight didn't need to sleep.

The deputy knocked on the doctor's door, but there was no answer. He knocked harder, and still no one came. Finally, Sheriff Durben pushed the deputy aside and went in.

"It's Sheriff Durben!" he yelled. "Are you here, Doc?"

Paul entered the room and switched on the light. When he saw the sheriff, he stretched and yawned.

"What's wrong?" Paul asked. "Do you want your money back?"

Paul rubbed his eyes and adjusted his robe.

"No, I don't want my money back," the sheriff said, taking off his coat. "I bumped my head. You can handle a bump on the head, can't you?"

Paul yawned and motioned with his hand to the sheriff.

"Sit down on the couch while I get my bag. Bump on the head, huh?"

The deputy looked at the sheriff, and then stationed himself by the door.

"Let me see that bump," Paul said. He sat next to the sheriff and smiled. "Ah, it's a big one, isn't it? I haven't seen one this size since Rufus tried to catch those chimney bricks on the fly. No, come to think of it this is the biggest one I've ever seen. How did it happen?"

The sheriff answered in an aggravated tone, "Rocks. Hard rocks. A lot of hard rocks happened."

Paul felt the bump, pressing his fingers deep into the sheriff's scalp.

The sheriff flinched. "Ouch! That hurt."

"Of course it hurt," Paul said. "I'm examining it."

"Then, don't examine it," Sheriff Durben replied, jerking his head back.

"Quit moving and be quiet," Paul insisted. "I know what I'm doing."

"I wish I did. Are you going to spend all night playing with my head?" Sheriff Durben asked.

"What's the problem?" Paul replied. "I didn't do this to you."

Paul reached into his bag for some antiseptic and cotton.

"I know you didn't," the sheriff grumbled. "A dog did it. And if I ever get my hands on that mutt, it's straight to the pound."

Paul smiled. "A dog did it?"

"If you must know," the sheriff answered grumpily, "I was investigating a stranger I spotted on the cliff above the grotto. I was climbing the trail when a small dog jumped on me, and I lost my footing and fell. End of story."

"Why didn't you have the stranger come down to you?" Paul asked.

"You trying to tell me how to do my job, Doc?"

"No. Only asking a question."

Paul moved his hand in front of the sheriff's face.

"Watch my finger," Paul said.

Paul looked into the sheriff's eyes and smiled. Durben pushed Paul's hand away and felt the bandaged bump.

"What's the verdict, Doc?"

"The medical term is booboo. You'll have a headache in the morning, but you should be fine otherwise. But, just to be on the safe side, I want you to stay here tonight. I don't think you have a concussion, but I want to be sure."

"I don't think that's such a good idea," Sheriff Durben said. "I'm kind of used to my own bed and my own company."

"It's only for one night. You'll hardly notice me."

"I don't know," Sheriff Durben moaned.

"If you're nervous, you can have the bedroom with the lock."

Paul smiled, but the sheriff wasn't amused.

"Well, I suppose I can tolerate your nagging until morning." Sheriff Durben turned to the deputy. "Thanks for your help. It looks like I'm staying here tonight."

"Anything you say, Sheriff," the deputy replied. "Will you be filing a report?"

"No, I won't be filing a report!" Sheriff Durben said. "It would be a little awkward to admit I was assaulted by an itty-bitty dog, now, wouldn't it? And I certainly wouldn't want to put it down on paper for the whole world to admire before the next election."

The deputy swallowed his smile and went to the door. "In that case, good night, Sheriff, Doctor Bradford."

Sheriff Durben took a cigar out of his pocket; Paul stared at him. Sheriff Durben grunted and put the cigar back.

"How about a couple of hands of poker before turning in?" Paul asked.

"No thank you. I've been rolled enough for one day."

# Chapter XVII

Sunday morning was sunny and bright, the temperature cold, and the wind crisp. Sheriff Durben was as snug as a bug in a rug, asleep on the couch in Dr. Bradford's living room. The bed was too soft, and he didn't like closed doors. His clothes were neatly folded on a chair, well within reach if the need arose. At ten past seven, the rays of the sun flowed through the window in a steady stream of light, forming a white, luminous pool around the sheriff's stoic face.

First one eye opened, then the other. A yawn followed. The sheriff sat up, stretched, and felt his head.

"Ouch," he said. "That blasted dog. I owe him one for this." The sheriff grabbed his pants. "I owe him two," he said, inspecting the cigar burn in one leg and a rip in the other.

As the sheriff got dressed, the incident ran through his mind. Then, the sheriff got an idea. Perhaps this Angelo fellow was once a wounded veteran like himself? If so, the veteran's hospital was the best place to start asking questions. The sheriff picked up Paul's phone and dialed the operator to get the number for the hospital. The phone at the hospital rang several times before it was answered.

"Hello?" the voice said. "May I help you?"

"Hello," Sheriff Durben replied. "I need to speak to someone in the administration office."

The sheriff was asked to wait while the call was transferred. A moment later the phone clicked and a man with a feeble voice spoke.

"Can I help you? I'm Mr. Miller."

"I'm Sheriff Durben. I'm calling from Mayfield, and I need some information."

"Exactly what kind of information do you need, Sheriff?"

"I need to know if anyone named Angelo has been recently discharged or, perhaps, wandered off in the past few days."

"I'm sorry, but no one named Angelo has been discharged from this facility or, as you say, has wandered off in the past few days. But you know, that name does ring a bell. Do you have a minute while I go through our records?"

"Go ahead, it's...my nickel."

While the sheriff waited he took a cigar from his pocket and rolled it between his fingers, testing its freshness. The cellophane wrapper crinkled, and the tobacco squished like a stiffened marshmallow. Satisfied that it was indeed fresh, and that Paul was nowhere around, he removed the wrapper.

He placed the cigar securely between his teeth and reached into his pocket for a match, but there were none to be found.

Mr. Miller returned. "Are you still there, Sheriff?"

"Yes, go ahead."

"I thought I recognized that name, but I wasn't certain. So many vets pass through here," he said. "We did have someone named Angelo. No." There was a long pause. "Now, I remember." There was another pause followed by a clearing of the throat. "I'm afraid I can't release this information."

"Why not?" Sheriff Durben asked.

"I can't tell you that either. I'm sorry, but only his attending physician, Dr. Behrman, can give you information from his file."

"Then, let me talk to him," Sheriff Durben said.

"He's making his rounds, but I can have him call you later."

"Never mind. I'll call back when I have time. Good-bye."

Paul entered the room and yawned. "Well, Sheriff," he said. "Whose money have you been spending on the phone?"

"Probably mine, if you must know," Sheriff Durben replied. "In any case, it was official business. I was checking on that stranger I saw at the grotto."

"Find anything out?"

"Yes and no. I have to call back and talk to some doctor." The sheriff took the cigar out of his mouth and rolled it between his fingers. "How about giving me a ride to my patrol car?"

"Sure. I'll drop you off on my way to church," Paul said. "You wouldn't want to join me, by any chance? A lot of voters will be there today to get a look at the new statue."

The sheriff put the cigar into his mouth, rolled it in his lips like a peppermint stick, and then spoke. "Church? Haven't you heard of the separation of church and state? And besides, you wouldn't want to give Reverend Richmann a heart attack, would you? Just take me to my patrol car."

"Maybe you're right." Paul scratched his whiskers and made a face as if tasting something bitter. "We'll leave as soon as I shave and brush my teeth. Last night's supper is still alive and well."

"You wouldn't happen to have a match?" Sheriff Durben asked.

"Try the glove box in my car," Paul answered. The sheriff stared at Paul, and Paul relented. "If you must light up, there's a book of matches in that desk drawer, just do it outside."

"Then, you better hurry up and get ready," Sheriff Durben insisted. "It's cold out there, and a cigar doesn't give off much heat."

"I'll only be a few minutes."

The cigar was half smoked when Paul emerged from the house wearing his new suit, favorite tie, and diamond stickpin.

"Dear God," the sheriff said. "What's that smell?"

"French cologne," Paul replied, adjusting his hat. "It was a gift from...an acquaintance."

"Acquaintance, huh?" The sheriff said with a grin. "Are you going to pray or court?"

"Probably both," Paul answered, smiling. "Let's go."

The ride was uneventful, but Sheriff Durben was anxious to get it over. The French cologne offended his nose. He preferred the smell of Old Spice, burning tobacco, and aged whiskey--all American made.

Sheriff Durben waved good-bye to Paul and walked over to his patrol car. The brimmed hat lay on the front seat. The sheriff turned toward the mountain.

"I wonder what he was doing up there?" he said aloud.

He felt the bandage on his head, cringed in pain, and slapped the top of the patrol car. When the pain left, he walked over to the grotto and searched for evidence of the previous day's misadventure.

The singing from St. Andrew Church filled the air and echoed off the face of the mountain. The sheriff's head, however, was throbbing to the thumping of a kettledrum. He was angry and determined to correct his earlier mistake. The lump on his head was an annoying reminder that someone else had escaped him.

The sheriff walked over to the spot where he had fallen. "Ah, there's my little friend's paw prints," he said aloud. "No doubt the brains behind the gang. And those must belong to his sidekick, Angelo."

Sheriff Durben followed the footprints back to the cave. He saw a hole in the rubble-filled entrance. A chill ran down his back. He knelt and peered into the opening, then reached into the hole and grabbed a leather-like object lodged inside.

"A strange place to lose a wallet," he said to himself. "At least it used to be a wallet." He opened it and found a photo of a woman carefully sealed between two sheets of clear plastic. "I wonder who she is?" Several boulders rolled down the face of the mountain and crashed on the ground a few feet away. "Time to leave," he said, looking upward. "The mountain is restless today, and I don't need another bump on my head."

A quarter mile beneath the sheriff's feet, men were working the mineshafts. The shafts were cold and damp and closer to hell than the pearly gates. A prayer would have had a hard time reaching the surface, let alone make its way to heaven. A song was seldom sung, but humming could sometimes be heard.

Rosey was fond of humming, particularly Christmas carols. Usually he started his serenade a few days before Santa's arrival. But this year he started on Thanksgiving and, judging by the strength of his voice, he seemed likely to continue his serenade through the feast of the three kings. The men didn't mind; they certainly wouldn't complain. They just wondered why. Everyone assumed it was because of her, whoever she was.

"Rosey," one miner asked, "when are we going to meet your girlfriend?"

Rosey ignored the miner's question and inspected the repair work that had been done on some of the timbers in shaft number four.

"C'mon, Rosey, tell us something about her," another miner pleaded.

"Why is it any concern of yours?" Rosey answered.

Rosey was somewhat red in the face and didn't want to continue the present conversation.

"Cause, we want to see the woman who can turn a Po-lack into a canary," the miner joked.

Rosey stared at the miner, and the joke died.

"This Polish canary is going to start crowing real quick if you don't start paying more attention to your work." Rosey placed his hand on some loose shoring and shook it. Dirt and chunks of coal fell from the ceiling. "I want this reinforced before you go any farther."

"Will do, chief," the men said in harmony.

Rosey shook his head and hopped into one of the rail cars heading for the surface, humming all the louder. Steven was at the entrance talking to one of the engineers. When he saw Rosey, he walked over to him.

"How's it coming?" Steven asked.

"I can't complain. Honeycut and his crew are doing a good job of clearing away the loose debris. If all goes well, we'll drill the blasting holes today and open the shaft on schedule."

"Are you still worried?" Steven asked.

"I worry about firecrackers on the Fourth of July. So, yeah, I'm worried." Rosey stretched and turned to face the sunlight peeking through the entrance. "But I must admit that the shaft is looking better than I expected, at least so far."

Steven let out a sigh of relief. "Good. I was beginning to have second thoughts." He put his hands into his pockets and walked Rosey to the exit. "If we fill these contracts, we'll be in the black for the first time in six months."

# Chapter XVIII

As Mary and her mom walked home from church, Mary's thoughts were of her dad--memories worn out from constant visitation. She missed his touch, his voice, and even the scent of his after-shave. Mary knew the separation was worse for her mother. Although her mother tried to hide it, Mary saw the yearning in her eyes for the part of her life called wife.

Mary opened the door to the house and stood at the threshold. She wanted to go home, not here. Not this hollow shell of a room filled with tears and dirty clothes.

"Mom, can I go to the park?"

Mary waited for an answer, and then repeated the question.

"Go to the park?" Cynthia asked, ushering Mary inside. "You can go after you finish your chores."

"But I'm late. Can't I do them when I get back? Please. Just this once?"

"Late for what?"

"I have to see someone."

"That someone wouldn't be Toby by any chance?" Cynthia asked. Mary bowed her head. Cynthia grinned. "If I didn't know better young lady, I'd think you were infatuated with that someone."

"In what?" Mary asked.

"If I wanted you to know, I'd say it plain and simple. You're not ready for what I'm thinking. Why all this sudden interest in the park?"

"It's the sledding championship today. Toby is going to be the world champion."

"He is, is he?" Cynthia took a deep breath. "I guess you're maturing faster than I thought." She smiled. Mary wondered why. "Sure, you can go. Why not? It doesn't get any more special than this. Just be back in time to finish your chores."

Mary changed her clothes and was on her way to the park in a matter of minutes. She ran as fast as her legs would carry her, stopping briefly along the way to fasten her boot buckles and button her coat. She was late and didn't want to miss Toby's victory.

The hill was ahead. The snow was deep, and a bottle was hidden beneath its frozen flakes. She stepped on it at full speed, flew into the air, and landed square on her back.

Footsteps pounded the snow as someone ran over to help. Mary lifted her head, then giggled and proceeded to make a snow angel.

"Are you all right, little girl?" Jeffrey asked.

He took her by the hand and she stood.

"I'm all right, Mr. Carston," Mary answered cheerfully. "I fell on an angel. See."

Jeffrey looked down. The wind swirled faster and faster until flake-by-flake the snow angel took flight. Mary, quick as a wink, ran into the whirling mist and turned in a circle with outstretched arms until she was covered from head to toe with glittering specs of white. But as swift as it came, the wind went away, taking the snow angel with it.

Mary skipped over to Jeffrey and said with a smile, "I never danced with an angel before."

"And I never saw a snow angel fly," he replied.

Jeffrey brushed the snow off Mary's coat and ran his fingers over the Silver Star pinned to her lapel.

He looked into her eyes and said, "Do I know you? You look very familiar."

"I'm a friend of Toby's."

"I'm afraid I don't know many of Toby's friends," Jeffrey said. "Which one are you?"

"I'm Mary, Mary Klein. Don't you remember? We rode together in Dr. Bradford's car."

Jeffrey's pocket watch chimed the hour. Jeffrey looked stunned. Mary's eyes widened as he took out the watch.

"That's a beautiful watch, Mr. Carston," Mary said.

"It was my father's and before him, his," Jeffrey answered. "My dad gave it to me when I took over the bank."

"I knew your dad," Mary said, energetically. "He liked candy. One day, when Mom and me were at the bank, he gave me some. He told me to always remember that life is better when you have a pocket filled with butterscotch candy." Jeffrey had a blank expression. His eyes watered. "Are you all right, Mr. Carston," Mary asked.

Jeffrey smiled in a slow, delightful manner.

"I am now," he answered. He reached into his coat pocket. "Here," he said. "Have some. They're my favorite, too."

"Thank you, Mr. Carston." Mary unwrapped the candy and popped it into her mouth. "That's really good candy. Can I have one for Mom?"

"Here," Jeffrey said. "Have a handful."

Mary filled her pocket, then turned and pointed to the hill. "There's Toby," she said. "We better hurry, or we'll miss his run."

Toby and Bailey were standing nose to nose. In the past, each gladiator had challenged the mighty oak and won. Today, the opponent was made of flesh and blood. A hush came over the spectators as if decreed by the shrill whistle of a referee. The two sleds were prepared; the run was cleared. The witnesses lined the side of the hill. The time was right for someone to strike the mortal blow and declare victory.

The oak waited with rooted defiance. Bailey was first to accept the challenge. He grabbed his sled, ran to the edge of the hill, and dove into the air with all the reckless abandonment of the knights of old charging the Saracens at the towering, Jerusalem gates.

It didn't look like he would ever come down when suddenly the sled hit the ground with a terrible thump that nearly knocked Bailey off. But he held on tight and steered a true course, following the tracks of his previous runs.

Someone yelled, "Turn! Turn! Turn! You're going to hit the tree!"

But Bailey ignored the warning and continued his charge. He was a breath away when he pulled on the rudder and swerved to the right, missing the tree by half an inch.

"I've won!" he shouted, bringing his sled to a stop. "I've won," he said, pointing to Toby.

"Not yet, you haven't," Toby yelled. "Not by a long shot."

Toby kicked the snow and looked at his dad and Mary. His expression was resolute. Mary waved. She knew he would win or crash trying. She feared the worst as Toby lifted Old Red high in the air and ran to the edge of the hill.

He launched himself skyward like a fourth of July rocket. Old Red and Toby were as one. They hit the ground with a thunderous report, Old Red's rudders tracking deep into the snow, running swift and true like a bolt of lightning, rumbling, roaring, and striking between heartbeats. Mary feared all was lost. Toby was going too fast, and the tree was too close. But at the last moment, Toby shifted his weight, hooked his foot under the deck, and then, just as Old Red was about to slam into the oak, he jerked the sled on its side and rode Old Red on one blade.

It was over in the blink of an eye. The mighty foe was struck a mortal blow, Old Red's mark left on the bark for all to see.

"Toby!" Mary cried out. "You did it!" She ran to him with open arms, but he was too quick, and she missed. "That was the greatest run ever," she said, lowering her empty arms.

"It was better than any in my day," Jeffrey said.

Bailey walked past and yanked on his sled rope.

"You win," Bailey said, grudgingly. "But I'm still the champ at cat's eyes marbles."

"Till next summer, anyway," Toby replied.

Jeffrey smiled and fingered his cat's eye marble fob. Mary scooted next to Toby.

"What do you want to do now?" Jeffrey asked Toby.

"I think I need to rest, Dad. That last run kind of took it out of me."

"Then, how about coming home for some of Mom's apple pie? I'm sure I can talk her out of one." Jeffrey put his hand on Toby's shoulder and looked at Mary. "Your friend is welcome to come along."

Mary tilted her head up. "Thank you for the invitation, Mr. Carston, but I have something important to do." Mary turned to Toby and whispered, "It's real important."

"Well, maybe next time?" Jeffrey said.

"Thank you, Mr. Carston." Mary chirped out the words like a bird. "I'd be happy to some other time."

Mary gave Toby the eye and a not-so-subtle nudge in the side. Signs he had experienced in the past, telling him she had something important she wanted him to do or had something earth shattering she wanted to say. It also told him that they had to be alone.

Toby turned to his father and said, "If it's all right with you, Dad, I'll walk Mary home, first."

"Of course it is," Jeffrey replied. "I'll put Old Red in the garage for the night."

"Thanks, Dad."

"No, thank *you*, son. And," Jeffrey added with a smile, "a good day to you, Mary Klein."

Jeffrey left with Old Red. Toby turned to Mary.

"What is it?" Toby asked in an irritated tone.

"I want you to come with me to meet someone."

"Who?"

"A man," Mary replied. "His name is Angelo."

Toby crossed his arms. "Who's he?"

"I'm not exactly sure. He's new in town."

"I know lots of people all ready," Toby said. "I don't want to meet anyone new."

"He knows magic," Mary whispered.

Toby's eyes widened. "Magic?"

"He learned it in Africa," Mary said.

"My uncle knows magic," Toby replied, smugly. "Shot a pea from his nose once while we were eating supper, but he's never been to Africa." Toby turned away. His dad was still in sight. Toby shuffled his boot in the snow. "Nah, I don't think I want to meet anther magician."

"Never mind," Mary said. She turned away and hung her head. "I better leave."

She walked slowly and looked back every now and then to see if Toby was watching.

"Wait a minute!" Toby yelled. He ran over to her and sighed. "I didn't say I wouldn't go. Anyway, I never met anyone from Africa."

# Chapter XIX

Mary led the way. Toby followed a few steps behind. Mary realized he didn't want to go, but she didn't want to go alone. She needed a witness if Angelo had good news, and help if things went badly. She also wanted Toby, more than anyone else, to believe in her and her family.

"How come this Angelo guy's hiding in the woods?" Toby asked.

"He's not hiding," Mary explained. "He just likes being alone with his thoughts, like one of them monks we studied about in school."

"Monks?" Toby said with a grimace. "Oh, you mean one of those guys that lives in a cave."

"That's a hermit," Mary said. "Monks don't live in caves, they live in monasteries where they pray and think about things."

"Maybe he just doesn't like people?" Toby said.

"He likes people; he just doesn't like mixing with towns-folk all the time, that's all."

"But, we're townsfolk," Toby reminded her.

Mary gave it some thought and answered, "Someone told me once that there are exceptions to every rule."

Toby grumbled, "I'll bet that someone never went into the woods looking for monks."

Mary followed her footprints of the previous day as best she could, but during the night the wind had blown a fresh layer of snow over the trail. Only the outline of a few scattered footprints remained.

The farther they went, the more apprehensive Toby seemed. His pace slowed until he finally stopped.

"Maybe he's crazy or something?" Toby said. "For all we know he could be an escaped convict or even a gangster."

Mary turned. Toby stepped forward.

"He's not crazy, or a gangster," she said. "He's a friend."

Mary walked in a small circle and surveyed the surrounding area. The place looked familiar, but she wasn't quite sure. Her old footprints were no longer visible, and the path came to a fork, something she didn't remember. While Mary decided which trail to take, Toby assumed the role of lookout, but other than one frightened rabbit, there was nothing to cause alarm.

The wind changed direction; Mary's hair swept across her face. She turned and caught the sweet scent of burning pine needles.

"I think he's over there," Mary said.

She pointed to the path that led through a heavy thicket. Toby sniffed the air and followed his nose until they came to a clearing in the center of which was a large campfire, but no one was there.

"I don't see him," Mary said.

"Maybe we should come back later?" Toby replied.

"No. Let's wait for him," Mary said. "I'm sure he'll be right back."

Toby stepped into the open; Mary stood by his side. The campfire cracked, and a small swirl of smoke escaped the flames and snaked along the ground in their direction. It circled Toby's feet, floated to his waist, then his chest, and finally his face. It was almost as if it had a mind of its own. It wouldn't leave until Toby, with Mary's help, fanned it away.

"Let's get closer to the campfire," Mary said.

"Wait a minute," Toby said, coughing.

They took two steps forward, but when they took the third, the campfire exploded in a huge ball of light that momentarily blinded them. When their vision cleared, Angelo stood in place of the light, his arms crossed like a genie freed from a bottle.

"Where did he come from?" Toby asked, rubbing his eyes.

"I don't know," Mary replied, "but I told you he was here, somewhere. Come on," she said. She pulled him by the hand. "He won't hurt us."

Toby's expression reflected his doubts. He walked over to the man but stopped several feet out of Angelo's reach. Mary wanted to get closer, but Toby wouldn't move.

"That was a mighty fine trick, mister," Toby admitted. "Mary told me you were some kind of a magician?"

"Trick?" Angelo said with a grin. "There's no trickery here, just a little science. But if its tricks you want, look over there."

Angelo pointed accusingly at a distant blackberry bush and said, "Come out of there, Agamemnon. Mary's friend wants to see a trick."

"My name is Toby, Toby Carston, if you please," Toby politely informed him.

"Bravely spoken," Angelo said with a nod. "And I am Angelo," he added, looking at Mary from the corner of his eyes, "if you haven't already heard. Now, on with the task at hand. Come here, Agamemnon. Toby Carston requests a trick."

A muffled whimper was heard as a small brown and white terrier emerged from the brambles. He shook his fur clean, scratched his ears, and trotted over to Angelo. Angelo snapped his fingers, and the dog sat. Angelo pointed his finger at the dog and scolded him for his laziness, then snapped his fingers again. Whereupon, the dog somersaulted, wagged his tail, and trotted over to the fire, turning his back to Angelo and spreading out on the ground like a bearskin rug.

Angelo's expression was one of disapproval. He turned to the children and said, "He's done better, but it's been a long day, and he's had little to eat. Still, that's no excuse for bad manners and poor showmanship."

Angelo stepped forward and reached out to shake Toby's hand. He towered over the boy like the oak on the sledding hill, but Toby's face revealed no fear. He raised his chin and extended his hand. After they shook, Angelo gave him a polite nod, and then sat down on a log situated in front of the campfire.

The dog wagged his tail and muffled a bark. Angelo patted the dog on the head. The little dog rolled on its back, and Angelo scratched its belly.

"All is forgiven," Angelo said. "Next time you'll do better."

Mary took a step toward Angelo, but Toby pulled her back. He preferred to sit on another log, the one opposite the stranger, putting the campfire between them. After the customary shy glances and smiles through the smoke, Mary got down to business. Her voice was animated and filled with anticipation.

"You told me that when I came back you'd tell me more about the bank robber."

Toby looked at Mary. He appeared confused and nervous. Mary gave him a reassuring smile.

Angelo scratched his head and said, "Did I?"

Mary looked at him, her eyes glared.

"You told me you would," she said.

Angelo stared at Toby and replied, "And I suppose Toby's your witness?" The campfire popped. Angelo turned and rubbed his knee. "I thought I told you to come back tomorrow?"

Mary crossed her arms and replied smartly, "It *is* tomorrow. That was yesterday."

"Is it?" Angelo asked. "It seems like today. And if that's the case, it can't be tomorrow."

The dog whimpered. Mary huffed.

"Today is yesterday's tomorrow," she said.

Angelo removed his stocking cap and scratched his head with his fingers. His white hair was thick and unruly and had to be forced back under the stocking cap.

"I'll have to take your word for that," he said. "One day is much like another to me."

He was about to continue, but something in the campfire caught his attention--a small tongue of fire colored red, blue, and green that seemed to have a life of its own. It floated above the rest of the flames, searching for something to burn. When Angelo bent down to examine it closer, the embers exploded, shooting hot slivers in every direction.

The dog jumped to his feet and ran away, his tale tucked between his legs. The firewood cracked, and the children jerked back. The little flame reached higher. Angelo took a deep breath to blow the flame out. But before he blew, the tiny flame withdrew, leaving Angelo with a mouth full of air and nothing to blow.

Angelo looked at the children and swallowed.

Mary giggled. Toby and Angelo laughed.

"It doesn't take much to amuse me these days," Angelo confessed. "You'd think the less you had, the sadder you'd be, but I find the opposite to be true."

An owl hooted in the distance. It was a lonely call, or so it seemed to Mary. She looked at Angelo and wondered if he too was alone in the world. She wanted to ask him, but couldn't, not without crying.

Angelo looked at her; his expression was one of concern.

"The sheriff and I met yesterday under somewhat un-usual conditions," Angelo confessed. "It seems he knows my name. Strange. I don't remember being introduced."

Mary lowered her head and said, "I guess someone must have told him."

"And I'll bet that someone told someone else, who in turn told someone else. I must be quite a popular man by now."

"No you're not," Mary insisted.

Angelo chuckled. "So you say, and so I pray."

Mary took courage in his laughter and smiled.

"But what about the man who robbed the bank?" Mary asked.

"Oh, the bank robber. Didn't I tell you?" Angelo paused and rubbed his hands together over the fire. "He's dead."

Angelo's voice had no emotion and his face no expression.

Mary grabbed Toby's hand.

"He's dead?" she asked.

"Dead and buried in the grotto cave, or so I believe. His name was Nolan James. It probably still is. Which poses an interesting question: Will he always be Nolan James?" Toby looked at Mary. He had a sour expression and was about to speak. Mary shook her head no, and Angelo continued. "Be that as it may, if someone tells someone and that someone tells the sheriff, he'll probably dig Nolan out, and your father will go free."

Mary squeezed Toby's hand. Toby freed himself from her grasp and whispered into her ear, "How do we know he's telling us the truth? He could be making this whole thing up."

Mary stared at Angelo through the smoke. He faded in and out like the flickering light of a wavering neon sign turning itself on and off with a click and a clang and a spark and a flash.

The smoke cleared. Angelo pointed to Toby and said, "I'm telling you the truth, Toby Carston." His words were quick and sharp. "I wish I were not, because if

Nolan is found before I can get to him, I will lose my astrolabe forever."

Angelo threw a rock into the fire, and then poked the flames violently with a stick.

Toby whispered, "Astrolabe?"

Mary replied softly, "I'll explain later." She turned to Angelo. "We believe you," she said. "Please don't be mad."

Angelo paused and laid the stick in the fire. As the stick burst into flames, his angry face softened and sadness settled in.

"I'm not angry at you, children. My anger stems from what may be, and from what's beyond my control."

"Come on. Let's go," Toby said.

Toby gave Mary's coat sleeve a tug.

"Just a little while longer," she begged.

"He's starting to worry me," Toby replied.

Mary asked Angelo what was wrong. Angelo's eyes widened; his muscles tensed, his voice alarmed.

"I fear that terrible things will happen. Last night I overheard some miners talking outside the diner. They said they are going to use explosives to open one of the shafts sometime around five o'clock Christmas eve, the shaft that runs beneath that mountain, my old camping grounds," he said, pointing. "If they do, I fear that some of people attending the performance at the grotto may be injured, perhaps even die."

A heavy, frigid mist dropped from the trees, covered the children and nestled the campfire like a hen an egg. Mary shivered. The fire retreated, and the red embers turned gray. Angelo stirred the dying ash with a stick, and the fire came back to life.

"I don't understand," Mary said.

She looked at Toby. Toby turned to Angelo.

"What are you talking about?" Toby asked.

Angelo's answer was sadly spoken. "The explosion in the mine could cause a landslide."

"Landslide?" Mary asked.

"I told you the mountain wasn't safe. The earthquake tremors, remember? They've weakened the overhanging cliff. When the explosion goes off, the cliff will slide down the mountain," he said, pointing at Toby, "like your sled down the hill. It will crush everything in its path."

"Are you sure?" Toby asked.

"As sure as I can be," Angelo replied. "And that's one-hundred percent certain."

Angelo picked at his scraggly beard as if an idea were concealed inside. Toby looked at Mary with a concerned expression. Mary sighed and looked at Angelo.

"Can't anything be done?" she asked. "There must be something we can do?"

"Change the time of the concert," Angelo answered, "or the time of the explosion or, better still, cancel them both."

"We can tell the sheriff," Toby said.

Mary shook her head. "I can't do that. He thinks we're thieves."

"Nor I," Angelo replied. "I would if I could, but I can't. He'd put me in jail and throw away the key for assault and battery or, at the very least," he said, turning to Agamemnon, "an accessory before and after the fact." Angelo raised his hands over the fire and rubbed them together. "If something isn't done, perish they will." He pointed at the children. "It's up to you! It's action we need!"

Angelo reached into his pocket and threw something into the campfire. The flames exploded with a loud pop--a ball of fire shot into the sky, and a shower of silver sparks sprayed the ground. The little dog howled, and the children jumped to their feet.

Angelo stood and squawked like a crow, "Shoo! Shoo! Be off, you two. Enough has been said. There's work to do."

He clapped his hands, and the children ran. They didn't stop until they reached the sledding hill.

# Chapter XX

Toby and Mary sat on a wooden crate that had outlived its usefulness as a sled. Toby seemed uneasy. He kept looking around as if someone was sneaking up on him.

Mary was thinking about what Angelo had said. Part of her wanted to jump for joy, part of her wanted to cry.

Toby turned to her and said, "I never really thought your dad did it. He was too happy to do something that would make others so sad."

"I'm glad you think so. I wish others did."

"They will when they find this Nolan guy buried in the cave."

"I hope they find your dad's money there," Mary said.

"That would make everything all right," Toby replied. "Even Mr. Daryl at the mine would be happy. He was at our house the other day talking business, like always. I don't think things are going good for him."

"Mr. Daryl?" Mary asked, curiously. "I saw his daughter at the general store last month. She's pretty, and kind of grown, isn't she?"

"Grown?" Toby asked.

"You know, filling out."

"I suppose," Toby replied. "I don't see her much. She goes to some fancy, private school in Charleston. Mr. Daryl told my dad that she might go to our school next year. I think because of money problems."

Mary's eyes narrowed. "But if they find the money, she can stay at that private school, couldn't she?"

"I guess so," Toby answered.

Mary grabbed her foot and moaned.

"What's the matter?" Toby asked.

"My foot is tingling."

"You probably sprained your ankle while you were running," he said. "Try rubbing it."

Mary removed her rubber boot and discovered a wet shoe and sock. She massaged her ankle and winced from the pain while Toby inspected her boot.

"Your boot has a hole in it," he said. "You can't go home like this. Your toes will freeze."

"You can give me a ride on your back, you're real strong," Mary replied.

She removed her shoe and sock and massaged her cold foot and toes.

"I'm not that strong," Toby complained. "Maybe we can patch the hole with something."

"There's a torn cardboard box over there," Mary said. "We can tear off a piece and put it inside my boot."

"That won't last more than a few steps before it gets soaked," Toby said.

Toby sat, swinging the damaged boot between his knees. Mary felt a tear form in her eye and searched her pockets for the handkerchief Dr. Bradford had given her.

"What's that?" Toby asked.

Mary held up a small, plastic packet.

"It's my mom's rain cap. She gave it to me to wear to church one day. I must have forgotten to give it back."

"Let me see it," Toby said.

Toby handed Mary her boot and unfolded the plastic rain cap.

"I have an idea," he said. "If we wrap your foot in it, it won't get wet."

Mary smiled. "That's a good idea."

"But we still have to do something to warm your foot," Toby said. "Your toes are turning blue."

Toby took off his boot, removed his thick, woolen sock and handed it to Mary.

"You can use this," he said. "It doesn't stink."

The sock was warm and soft and couldn't have been grander if placed inside a glass slipper, instead of a wet shoe inside a patched, rubber boot. Mary was instantly transported to the ball in a carriage drawn by wishes and dreams. The orchestra played her favorite song as she danced cheek to cheek with her prince. Prince Charming, however, blew on his toes, gave them a rub, and put on his boot.

Mary and Toby looked at each other, and then turned away and stared at the snow.

"We have to do something," Mary said, "to stop the people from going to the grotto on Christmas Eve."

"What can *we* do?" Toby asked.

"I don't know," Mary said. She slumped forward and hugged her knees. "I could tell Rosey, but he's at work. If I tell my mom, she'll get mad. She told me to stay away from Angelo."

"Face it," Toby said. "We're doomed. No one is going to believe either of us and that's that."

He brushed the snow off his pants legs. Mary wiggled her toes inside of the plastic-wrapped, wool sock as she gave the problem some thought.

"If we could only get them to cancel the choir service, everything would be all right," Mary said.

"They won't cancel it without a good reason," Toby replied, "and we're not a good enough reason." Toby thumped the wooden crate with his hand. It emitted a hollow thud that caught his attention. He thumped it again and said, "Everyone wants to go to the grotto tomorrow to see the statue of baby Jesus and listen to the choir, and nothing is going to stop them."

"Statue of baby Jesus?" Mary asked.

"A beautiful statue." Toby said. "My dad took it over to the church in a wooden crate just like this one," he said, tapping the crate. "If we hide the statue, they won't have any reason to go to the grotto, will they? After Christmas, we can put it back."

"Hide it where?" Mary asked.

Mary scooted closer to Toby. A spark of a smile emerged.

"Someplace they can't find it," he answered.

Toby looked at Mary and frowned. Mary realized he wanted her to move over, but she was content to stay where she was. Finally, after a minute or two of fidgeting, Toby had an idea.

"My dad says if you take care of the big problems the details will take care of themselves, or something like that."

Toby nodded with a feeling of self-confidence.

"I don't know," Mary replied. "I heard someone say the devil lives in the details."

"No, he don't," Toby insisted. "He's burning in hell. I think we should just get the statue and worry about hiding it later. I'm sure we'll think of something when we get there. We can do it at noon tomorrow, right after lunch."

Mary looked at him. Her smile faded.

"I don't know," she said. "It's not going to be easy getting away. I'm supposed to help my mom tomorrow."

Toby took a breath and sighed.

"That's okay," he said. "I'm sure I can do it alone, somehow."

Mary reached for Toby's hand, but he moved it away.

"I'm sorry," Mary said. "I'll get away somehow. I promise."

"Cross your heart?" Toby asked.

"Cross my heart and hope to die," she replied, crossing her heart with her hand.

Their eyes met, and they smiled. Mary's face was aglow. She and Toby were officially a twosome, at least for the time being.

"Then, it's you, me, and Old Red," Toby said.

"Old Red?" Mary asked.

"It's a heavy statue, and it's in a wooden crate," Toby informed her. "We can't just carry it around like a sack of groceries. Someone might see it, then we'd really be in trouble."

"I didn't think of that," Mary said.

Toby stood, and Mary extended her hand to him. Toby hesitated, then grabbed hold and gave her hand a powerful pull--she sprung up like a Jack-in-the-box.

They stood face to face. Mary looked deep into his eyes. Her face was warm and aglow with a smile. Toby blushed and let go of her hand.

"Don't do that," he said.

"Don't do what?" she asked.

"What you're doing," he answered. "It makes me feel *icky*."

But as hard as she tried, the smile wouldn't leave or the glow recede, so they walked side by side, maintaining the proper non-hand holding distance all the way to Mary's house.

Mary stood at the door; she didn't want to go in.

"How about coming inside for a minute?" she asked.

Toby shuffled his feet. "I don't know. It's getting late."

"Just come in and say hello. If my mom sees you, she'll know we were together and won't ask me where I've been or what I've been doing. I don't want to answer any questions right now."

"Okay, but only to say hello," Toby insisted. "If I get home late, *my* mom will want to know why."

The door creaked open with the sound of rusty hinges. The room smelled of laundry detergent and boiled chicken. The motor of one of the wringer-washers was chugging like a locomotive under the strain of a full load, as the agitator sloshed back and forth in a tub filled with soapy water. Piles of dirty clothes lay on the floor waiting their turn in the baptismal. Mary's mom was at the stove, stirring a pot of soup and humming a Christmas carol. But the sadness in her heart took all the joy out of the song. It was an empty shell of rhythmic notes dangling in the air like wilted flowers in a cracked vase. Mary wanted to tell her mom the good news, but couldn't. Mary believed Angelo, but she questioned whether something this good could really happen to them. Why get her mom's hopes up and get herself in trouble. They waited this long; they could wait a little while longer.

Cynthia turned and said, "Why hello, Toby."

"Hello, Mrs. Klein," Toby replied.

"Are you staying for dinner?" she asked.

"I can't stay today, Mrs. Klein. Me and Mary was just sledding and things, and I thought I'd walk her home."

Cynthia smiled and said, "That was very considerate of you."

"It's nothing," Toby said. "Well, she's home so I guess I'll go."

"Tell your mom hello for me," Cynthia said.

"I will, Mrs. Klein."

Mary walked Toby outside. They agreed to meet the next day at the bank. From there, they would go to St. Andrew Church and save the day.

∽◦∾

Toby ran home as fast as he could. He had to get Old Red out of the garage before his dad closed the heavy overhead door. Fortunately, when he peeked into the window, he saw his dad helping his mom prepare the dining room for the next day's activities. There was a table to set, chairs to move, and several odd jobs that had been put off too long. It gave Toby plenty of time to retrieve Old Red and hide him behind the woodpile.

He was on his way back to the house when a car pulled into their driveway. It was his uncle and aunt from Kentucky. They came bearing gifts.

Toby opened the back door, took off his coat, boots, one sock, and then waited in the mudroom until his mom left the kitchen. When she was gone, he walked casually into the living room as if nothing had happened. His uncle and aunt were talking to his dad and didn't notice his sudden appearance, which suited him just fine. He was more interested in the new gifts under the tree. After seeing his name on the appropriate number of boxes, he looked at his dad.

His dad was smiling, really smiling, and appeared to be enjoying himself. Toby didn't understand the changes taking place in his parents. This wasn't the same dad he had known for the past year. As for his mom, well, she was also smiling an awful lot lately and for no apparent reason.

Life was getting complicated. Toby shrugged and followed his nose to the kitchen. His mom was at the stove, basting a ham.

"Who's your dad talking to?" she asked.

She covered the ham and slid it into the oven. The oven door slammed with a loud metal clang, interrupting Toby's thoughts.

"Huh?" Toby answered.

"I said, who's in the living room with Dad?"

"Oh. It's only Aunt Stella and Uncle Lou. They brought over some Christmas presents."

"And an appetite, I'll wager." Marge removed her apron and laid it across a chair. "I thought they'd be stopping by. Oh well, two more mouths to feed today and two less tomorrow." Marge smiled and stirred one of the pots simmering on the stove. "You better go wash your hands. We'll be eating in a few minutes. Your Uncle Lou is not one for waiting."

Toby noticed that his mom had the same look as the ham, honey-glazed. He came to the conclusion that this was his house, but apparently not his parents. At least, not the ones he had before going to sleep the previous night. They were smiling, humming, didn't ask him any of the usual questions, and they had that *icky* look. He didn't know what was going on, but he didn't want it to change.

# Chapter XXI

Sunset came without fanfare or notice--a bleak, gray sky turned black. Most of the people in town were at the supper table or seated in a comfortable chair in front of the radio. Sheriff Durben, as usual, was on patrol. He cruised the town and observed the people, his people. At times like this, he was content with his place in the scheme of things and felt more like the town crier, who kept everyone informed of the news and correct time, rather than the dreaded enforcer of the law, who kept everyone secure and everything in order. His only uneasiness came when he thought about the stranger at the grotto. He wouldn't be able to enjoy Christmas until he discovered who this stranger was, and what he was doing in Mayfield. When he was confident that all was as it should be in town, he drove to his office and telephoned the veteran's hospital.

"Hello," Sheriff Durben said, "is this Mr. Miller?"

"Yes it is. Is this Sheriff Durben?"

"Yes. Is Dr. Behrman there?" the sheriff asked.

"You're in luck, Sheriff. Dr. Behrman is in the office next door. Hold on while I go get him."

The sheriff sat behind his desk and searched several of the drawers for a match to light his cigar. He was about to go over to the filing cabinets and continue his quest there, when the doctor spoke on the telephone.

"Hello? Are you still there, Sheriff?"

"I'm here. Is this Dr. Behrman?"

"It is. Mr. Miller told me about your inquiry, but as he informed you, patient files are confidential."

"How do I get it opened?" the sheriff asked.

"It usually requires a court order."

"You said usually." Sheriff Durben paused to take a breath. "I don't have time for that. Is there another way?"

"Not normally. However, I was Angelo's tending physician. And, under the circumstance, I may be able to tell you what you need to know without breaking patient confidentiality. Do you know Sheriff Clay?"

"I thought he retired?"

"He did, but his wife got tired of him lying around the house all day, so she pestered him back to work. I'll have him call you to verify your identity, and then I'll see what I can do for you."

"Sounds good to me, Dr. Behrman. I'll be in touch."

The sheriff put the phone down and yawned. It was time to call it a day and go home, although the prospect had little appeal. There was no one waiting for him, which to his way of thinking wasn't all that bad, but keeping his own company was less than desirable. He thought about getting a cat, but they make too many demands on the people they keep. A fish might be nice, but changing the water was too much like changing a baby's diaper. He liked dogs, but apparently they didn't like him. So, alone he was, and alone he would probably stay.

He grabbed the file folder containing the information on the bank robbery and left the office. He had read it numerous times, but there was always something new, something he hadn't noticed before, if only a misspelled name, a wrong date, or an ambiguous word he could have misunderstood.

When he got home, he was determined to go through the folder again--line by line if necessary--until he found that something he had overlooked the last time he reviewed it. But as hard as he tried, he couldn't find anything new.

It was just before dawn when he quit, his eyes burned and his stomach rumbled. He grabbed a handful of crackers, poured himself a cup of coffee, and walked over to the front porch window. The sidewalks and streets were deserted, the sky a dark-gray. The moon was departing, the morning star by its side. He smiled and made a wish. A foolish thing he thought, but he was out of leads and wanted help, no matter the source. He needed something, anything to point him in the right direction. Then, he remembered the hat.

A few blocks away, Cynthia stood at her kitchen window. The remnants of a spider's web clung to the outside window-pane. It sparkled in the rays of the rising sun like strands of spun crystal. Cynthia recalled the day the spider arrived. It was a warm Monday in May, just after she and Mary returned from visiting Sylvester. She remembered the first few strands of silk the spider spun, the repairs the spider made after each storm, and the life and death struggles that ensued. The spider departed with the arrival of the first frost. Where the spider went, she didn't know. She asked herself if it would survive the winter and return in the spring. She hoped it would.

Cynthia walked over to the bedroom door and looked at the lump moving listlessly under the blanket on Mary's bed.

"It's time for breakfast, sleepy head," Cynthia said. "We have a lot to do today."

Mary curled into a ball; her face buried in the pillow, and her voice muffled. "Just ten more minutes, Mom. Please?"

"It was ten minutes five minutes ago," Cynthia replied.

She walked into the bedroom and stood in front of the chifforobe mirror. She didn't particularly like what she saw staring back at her--a tired, lonely woman, aging with worry before her time. She put on a rehearsed smile and brushed her hair.

"It's going to be a busy Christmas Eve," she said, "and we need to get started."

Mary's voice was suddenly filled with energy as her head emerged from the blankets.

"It's Christmas Eve?"

"It's the day before Christmas," Cynthia replied, jokingly.

She looked at Mary's reflection in the mirror. Mary kicked back the blankets, sat on the edge of the bed, and wiped the sleep from her eyes. After a healthy yawn and lengthy stretch, Mary reached under her pillow to retrieve something. From the deliberateness of her actions and the look on her face, Cynthia assumed she was searching for something wiggly and slimy.

"It's here," she said in a voice barely above a whisper. "It wasn't a dream."

"What's that?" Cynthia asked.

"Nothing important, Mom. It's just a sock."

Cynthia shrugged and shook her head. She wasn't up to any new mysteries, so she let the subject drop. She took one last look into the mirror and laid the hairbrush down. She wondered if Sylvester would still find her attractive when he finished serving his time in prison. Her heart told her that he would, but her eyes weren't sure.

"Come on, your breakfast is getting cold," Cynthia said.

She went into the kitchen and sat at the table. Mary followed. She smiled and walked as if she were on a cloud.

"You're awfully cheerful this morning," Cynthia said. "Perhaps you'll share your secret with me?"

Mary gave her mom a hug and a kiss.

"I just feel good, that's all."

"Well, I have a surprise for you," Cynthia replied.

A small grin made its appearance on Cynthia's face. Mary sat and looked at the gift on the table next to the tree.

"It sure has a pretty ribbon and bow," she said.

Mary touched the wrapping paper as if it were made of butterfly wings. She wanted to pick it up and give it a shake, but decided to save that pleasure for Christmas morning.

"You have another surprise as well," Cynthia said. "It's in the chifforobe. When you're finished eating, you can go see."

Cynthia sipped her coffee and watched Mary eat her oatmeal and gulp down her glass of milk. As soon as Mary was done, she hurried to the bedroom to see what secret the chifforobe held.

"They're beautiful," Mary said. "You mean all these are mine?"

"They certainly are," Cynthia replied.

Mary grabbed the new dress, coat and hat all at once and hugged them. She stood in front of the mirror admiring her new clothes. She didn't know what to try on first.

"Thanks, Mom."

"Don't thank me. Thank that admirer of yours, Rosey." Cynthia finished her coffee and joined Mary in the bedroom. "He brought them over late last night on his way to work. He said his girlfriend helped pick them out." Cynthia paused. "I didn't know he had one. He also mentioned something about a princess, but I didn't understand a word he was saying." Cynthia stroked Mary's hair and smiled. "Make sure you thank him."

"I will, Mom. I've never had a dress this nice. It's exactly like the one in Miss Mae's store window."

"Indeed it is," Cynthia replied. "Rosey's friend certainly has good taste. You're going to be the prettiest girl at the hall tonight."

Mary held the dress up and said, "I hope it fits."

Cynthia pressed the dress against Mary's body to measure its length and gave the sleeves a tug.

"I think it will fit just fine," Cynthia said. "Why don't you try it on."

Cynthia smiled and remembered her first special dress. It wasn't that long ago, as far as time is counted, but an eternity if measured by feelings.

"What do you think, Mom," Mary said, turning in a circle.

"You look beautiful, my dear. Simply beautiful." Cynthia's voice quivered; her eyes were glassy. "That dress certainly brings out the blue in those big eyes of yours. If only your dad could see you."

Cynthia walked to the kitchen sink. Mary followed.

"What's wrong, Mom?"

"Nothing."

Cynthia turned on the tap and rinsed some dishes. A tear ran down her face. She wiped it away and forced a smile.

"How about bringing me your new coat," Cynthia said. "I need to brush it."

Mary rested her head against her mom's side.

"Mom, remember what you told me Pastor Amos said about a miracle? Well, there's going to be one. At first, I thought it might not happen, but now, I know it will."

"What in the world are you talking about?" Cynthia asked.

She dried her hands and ran her fingers through Mary's hair.

"I can't tell you right now, Mom."

"Another one of your secrets?"

"Kind of," Mary replied.

Cynthia kissed Mary's forehead.

"Take the dress off so I can iron it. While I'm doing that, you clean yourself up and get ready to go over to the hall to help with the decorations. There's a lot to do this morning and few hands to do it."

Mary looked at her mother and smiled.

"Mom, can I go out for a little while when we get back from the hall? I have to see Toby about something."

"Is it something I need to know about or just something in general?"

"Kind of both, Mom. Can I go, please?"

Cynthia had an uneasy feeling deep inside her stomach, but she didn't know why. Consequently, she wanted to say no. But when she saw the joy in Mary's face, she couldn't. Mary was happy, the happiest she had been in months. Cynthia wasn't about to change that, especially the day before Christmas.

"I tell you what," Cynthia said. "When we get back from the hall, you can go visit Toby for awhile, but only for a short while, mind you. I want you to come with me when I take the bean soup over to the hall. You can make yourself useful lifting and moving the heavy pots and pans and dishes. Some of the ladies are getting on in age, and I'm sure they would appreciate your help. Do we have a deal?"

"It's a deal, Mom."

# Chapter XXII

The bump on Sheriff Durben's head throbbed to the beat of his knuckles knocking on St. Andrew Church's parsonage door. While he waited for the sound of footsteps and the turning of the doorknob, he extinguished his cigar on the sole of his shoe, placed the cigar into his shirt pocket for later use, fanned the cloud of smoke away, spat out a bit of tobacco that was lodged between his teeth, and practiced his smile. These preparations complete, he secured the paper bag he held under his arm, stood at attention, and waited for the inspection.

The door opened, and Sheriff Durben gave Reverend Richmann a hearty hello. The reverend, however, was tongue-tied. He stared at his guest as if he were a mirage, then took the sheriff by the arm and pulled him inside. Sheriff Durben cleaned his shoes off on the hand-braided rug in the foyer, but only after a long hesitation. The ceremonial cleansing could signal a prolonged stay.

"I hope I'm not disturbing you, Reverend?" Sheriff Durben asked. "I won't be long."

"Stay as long as you like," the reverend replied. "May I take your coat?"

"That's all right, I'll keep it on."

The reverend's face showed his disappointment.

"What brings you here?" Reverend Richmann asked. He smiled; his eyes twinkled. "Membership is free, you know."

Sheriff Durben cleared his throat. "I'm here on official business," he said.

"Official?" the reverend said. "Well, at least you're here," the reverend joked. "How may I help you?"

Reverend Richmann put his hand on the sheriff's back and escorted him into the study as if the sheriff were a fragile porcelain doll that would break into a thousand pieces if he tripped and fell.

"I have something I want you to look at," the sheriff said. The reverend's close proximity was somewhat disturbing, so the sheriff skillfully maneuvered himself to a distance more suited his religious neutrality. "I'm hoping you might be able to shed some light on it for me."

"Shedding light is part of my job," the reverend explained.

Sheriff Durben suddenly realized that Reverend Richmann's study appeared to have more books than the town library. All the walls but one were lined with bookshelves that extended from the floor to the ceiling. They were filled with volumes on every subject from aardvarks to zymosan. There were also two reading tables with opened books on them, as well as some reference material scattered about the room on various chairs. The reverend apparently liked to read more than one book at a time, and it seemed that he liked to have one waiting for him at whatever location he happened to be present.

The reverend's wife entered the room. She gave Sheriff Durben a second look before she spoke. "I thought I heard voices. Can I bring you some coffee and perhaps a few oatmeal cookies?"

"Sounds good to me," Reverend Richmann said. He looked at the sheriff. "Surely you have time for one cup of coffee and a cookie or two?"

"I guess I have time for one cup, but no cookies, thank you," Sheriff Durben said. He knew he couldn't eat just one, and he didn't want to stay long enough to eat two or three.

"Then, if you'll excuse me," the reverend's wife said with a nod, "I'll be back in a minute with the coffee."

"While we're waiting," Reverend Richmann said, "why don't you unbutton your coat and sit on the couch? It's old but comfortable."

Sheriff Durben reluctantly did as requested. Reverend Richmann cleared his throat and sat in the chair across from the sheriff. The coffee table was between them, neutral ground to the sheriff's way of thinking.

Reverend Richmann looked at the paper bag and scratched his chin.

"How may I be of assistance?" he asked.

"You can tell me if you recognize this."

Sheriff Durben reached into the bag and pulled out the hat Angelo had placed under his head at the grotto.

He straightened the brim and spun the hat on his hand.

Reverend Richmann looked puzzled.

"A hat?" Reverend Richmann asked. "It does look familiar, but a lot of men in town wear a hat like that, especially on Sundays." The sheriff rubbed the bump on his head and flinched. The reverend leaned forward. "Are you feeling well?" he asked.

"It's just a little headache," Sheriff Durben replied.

"Can I get you an aspirin?"

"No thanks. It only lasts a second or two."

The reverend's wife entered, all smiles.

"Here's the coffee, and some homemade cookies in case you change your mind, Sheriff Durben."

The reverend stood and helped his wife put the serving tray on the table, and then he and his wife sat.

"Where did you get that hat?" Reverend Richmann asked.

The sheriff gave his answer some thought.

"A man left it at the grotto. I wanted to ask him some questions when I was interrupted. Well, anyway, I'm trying to find out who this guy is. I thought this might be a clue."

"Cream or sugar?" the reverend's wife asked.

"Black, if you please," Sheriff Durben replied.

The three quietly sipped some coffee for a moment. Sheriff Durben moved the hat closer to the reverend.

"Reverend, please look at the hat again. I don't know anyone in town who wears a brown hat with a dark-green headband. Are you sure it doesn't ring a bell?"

The reverend stared at the hat as he sipped his coffee. Suddenly, he took a large gulp, walked over to a desk, and took something out of one of the drawers. When he returned, he placed a comic book on the table.

"Dick Tracy," the reverend said, sitting.

His wife grinned and bit into a cookie.

"Dick Tracy?" Sheriff Durben asked. "You lost me, Reverend."

"It's strange what captures your thoughts during stressful times," Reverend Richmann said, "like a bank robbery." He took another sip of coffee, and then continued. "The man who robbed the bank had a broad-brimmed hat like that, like Dick Tracy. Why I should think of a comic strip character at the time of the robbery is beyond me, but I did. Maybe I was relating it to one of the episodes." The reverend blushed; his wife grinned. Reverend Richmann chuckled, and then said, "Sometimes I need a break from the book mites, if you know what I mean."

"I'm afraid I do," Sheriff Durben said with a nod. "But I can't imagine why the hat's description didn't come out at the trial, and I didn't see it in any of the statements."

Reverend Richmann took a deep breath. "I guess because Jeffrey, the clerk and I were too busy staring down the barrel of the robber's gun to notice his hat." The reverend paused as if in thought. "And, of course, he was also wearing that red bandana over his face like some cowboy in one of those western movies they show in the cinema. You could hardly miss that."

"I suppose at a time like that a hat is, after all, just another hat," Sheriff Durben said. He paused and drank the last of his coffee. "And, of course, we had Sylvester."

The sheriff put his coffee cup on the table and asked the reverend's wife if he could use their telephone.

"Why certainly," she said. "Just stay there and I'll bring it to you. It has a long cord."

"Thank you. I won't be on it long."

The sheriff dialed the telephone. Someone answered on the first ring.

"Hello. May I help you?" the voice asked.

"Is that you, Dr. Behrman?" the sheriff asked.

"Yes, it is."

"It's me, Sheriff Durben."

Dr. Behrman paused. "Sheriff Clay told me he spoke to you and that everything seems to be in order. Do you remember what he said?"

"He said you were moving to Arizona next month to be close to your son."

"So I am," Dr. Behrman said. "What can I tell you about Angelo?"

"Everything you can."

"Our records show that in his civilian life Captain David Angelo was a geology professor at the University of Montana. He enlisted in the army in January 1942 and was transferred here for treatment on November 18, 1943 along with several other patients from England. According to his service record he was assigned to the British $8^{th}$ Army in June of 1942 to help build roads and landing strips in preparation for the North African campaign. He was reported missing-in-action the following August, but was found several months later in a Bedouin camp that had been destroyed by the Germans. He was the only survivor, and in critical ccndition when he arrived at the British field hospital. They did what they could for him there, and then sent him to a hospital in Malta for surgery and additional treatment.

"According to their records, he suffered severe head trauma and had shrapnel wounds to his chest and abdomen. Besides that, he had a broken right leg with a shattered knee, and was unconscious for the better part of a month." The doctor paused. "When he arrived here, he was still in pretty bad shape, though not critical. I was, however, concerned about his mental state. He was very depressed, and he wouldn't eat. I was told that he received a letter telling him that his wife had died while he was in Africa, pneumonia I think. Then, several weeks later, his personal belongings arrived, and he just snapped out of it. If I had to guess why, I'd say it was because of that strange tote sack of his and not because of anything I did." The doctor paused. "He wouldn't let that sack out of his sight for even a minute. Of course, we were all curious about its contents. Finally, one night when he wanted to go outside and talk to the stars, as he was fond of saying, he let us in on its secret, an astrolabe. It was an ancient instrument and probably very valuable." The doctor paused and his voice became solemn. "He once told me that the astrolabe was his bridge to heaven and to his wife--sharing a space in time is how he put it. Oh well, I guess we all have our dreams. Don't we Sheriff?"

There was a moment of silence before the sheriff answered. "Is that all you can tell me?" he asked.

"Let's see." Dr. Behrman took a deep breath. "After Captain Angelo recovered, we started his physical therapy. Unfortunately, his right leg wouldn't mend, and our surgeon had to operate and put a pin in it. We couldn't do much about the knee. I might add that Angelo was a very likeable and knowledgeable individual. I enjoyed his company immensely."

Sheriff Durben's expression showed a hint of disappointment.

"Can you give me a description?" he asked.

"He was tall, about six-feet-two. He had dark eyes and hair the color of cotton, but he's not your man. He couldn't be." Dr. Behrman cleared his throat. "He died last year, killed by another patient a month or so before Christmas."

"Are you kidding me, Doc?"

Sheriff Durben looked at the phone.

"Are you still there, Sheriff?" Dr. Behrman asked.

"I'm still here."

"Let me explain. We had a mental patient here named Nolan James. He was delusional and quite unpredictable. He tried to escape on several occasions. One night he succeeded. On his way out, he pushed Captain Angelo down a flight of stairs and assaulted one of our security officers. I was told Captain Angelo died the following day of his injuries. I was on vacation at the time, so I don't know any of the finer details. As for Nolan, he reportedly lost control of the car during a police chase and drove into the river and drowned. His body was never recovered."

"I'm afraid all you've done is confuse me," Sheriff Durben said. He looked at Reverend Richmann and his wife. "Can you tell me what Nolan looked like?"

"Him, I will never forget. I still have a scar on my arm from one of his bites." Dr. Behrman paused. "Well, he was about my height, so that would make him about five-foot-eight. He was roughly 160 pounds, had curly dark-brown hair and green eyes. An average looking guy, you might say, for a psychotic."

"Do you remember if he had any identifiable marks like tattoos or scars?"

"No, nothing like that," Dr. Behrman said with a slight cough. "Only those gold teeth. Several molars, I believe."

"Gold teeth, you say?" The sheriff asked.

"Does that help?" the doctor asked.

"Perhaps," Sheriff Durben replied.

"Well, I'm afraid that's all the information I have." The doctor quietly chuckled. "Unless of course, you want to know about Agamemnon?"

"Who?" The sheriff asked.

"Agamemnon," Dr. Behrman repeated. "Perhaps I shouldn't have brought it up, but I can still see him jumping on his hind legs like a Pogo stick." Dr. Behrman chuckled again. "He was the patients' mascot, a small, brown and white terrier. He and Angelo were inseparable." The doctor's tone changed, and his voice betrayed his sadness. "He disappeared with...I mean, he disappeared after Captain Angelo's death."

The sheriff thought about what the doctor had just said. Something was suspicious.

"Dr. Behrman," the sheriff said, "is there something you're not telling me? It's important to my investigation that nothing be held back."

There were a few seconds of silence, then the doctor continued.

"You understand, Sheriff Durben, that what I'm about to tell you must be kept under the strictest of confidence?"

"I know the rules."

"Well, it so happened, the same week Captain Angelo died, we had two other fatalities, a rare occurrence I assure you. And to complicate matters, a terrible snowstorm closed all the roads. The funeral homes that had arranged to pick up the bodies couldn't get through, so we were forced to keep them in our morgue." The doctor hesitated. "When the hearses finally arrived, I was told that we were one body short, Captain Angelo's."

The sheriff was puzzled, and wondered if he had misunderstood the doctor.

"You lost a dead man?" the sheriff asked. His tone of voice was judgmental. The reverend and his wife looked at him. "He couldn't have just up and walked away."

The doctor coughed and cleared his throat.

"Let's drop the subject," he said. "I'm certain it was just a mistake caused by all the bureaucratic paperwork we have to fill out. Also, the administrator was new. Anyhow, I don't think it's relevant to your investigation."

"Relevant?" the sheriff said. "I'll be the judge of what's relevant. I have a robbery to solve, and your missing dead man might be involved."

The phone went momentarily silent.

"Hello," Sheriff Durben said. "Are you still there?"

"If there's nothing else," the doctor replied, hurriedly. "I'm afraid I must go. I have to make my rounds."

"Just one more thing," Sheriff Durben said. "What kind of clothes did this Nolan guy wear?"

Sheriff Durben could hear the doctor grumble under his breath.

"I believe Nolan stole Angelo's civilian clothing," the doctor said in a calmer voice. "Angelo tried to stop him, and that's when Nolan pushed him down the stairs."

"Did either Angelo or Nolan wear a hat?" Sheriff Durban asked.

"I don't know. Angelo was on his own most of the time. I only saw Nolan during his examinations. If that's all, Sheriff, I have to get back to my patients."

"I guess that'll be it, Doctor. If something comes up, I'll give you a call."

The reverend's wife walked over to Sheriff Durben, and he handed her the phone.

"Thank you," he said.

"You're more than welcome," she replied.

Sheriff Durben put the hat back into the paper bag, stood, and buttoned his coat.

"Thanks for your time and help, and for the wonderful coffee...and cookies," he said, reaching into the serving tray.

"Must you go so soon?" the reverend's wife asked.
"Yeah, people might start to talk."

# Chapter XXIII

oby was in a fix. He had to keep his rendezvous with Mary, but he had a house filled with relatives observing their annual get-together. His mom was in the kitchen, cooking; her two sisters were in the parlor rearranging the chairs and setting the tables. His dad was in the study discussing his cousin's next gubernatorial campaign. Beneath the Christmas tree were a multitude of brightly wrapped gifts. Moving around the tree, like Indians circling a covered wagon, were several youngsters inspecting the gifts. Two of the boys shook the boxes like rattles, a third just stood and stared. A toddler chewed on one of the bows, a girl in a blue velvet dress stacked some gifts one on top of the other while another girl sat on the floor, jiggled a box, and hugged it when it emitted the word, "Mommy." Toby's Cousin Todd was waiting for the right time to make his move. He and Toby didn't get along even on the happiest of occasions.

Toby bent over to read the name on a gift tag. Todd gave him a push, and the wrestling began, much to the annoyance of Aunt Lucille. She didn't get along with any two-legged instrument of the devil, as she was fond of saying. And, as expected, it didn't take long for her to scold the two rascals and threaten to report them immediately to their parents if they didn't stop roughhousing and settle down.

Toby and Todd retreated to neutral corners, and a type of peace and quiet returned to the room. But the other children soon filled the newly created void with their voices and laughter as they played a game of hide and go seek until they were called to dinner.

In the Carston family, it was a common practice for the children to eat in the parlor at these large get-togethers, separated from the adults in the formal dining room. The distinction between child and adult was apparently based on both the age and maturity of the child, although the parents always had the last word. A meal seasoned with tension was always distasteful to the adults. As a result, the children had to fend for themselves with only minimal parental interference.

This separation from the parents gave Toby an opportunity to slip out of the house. If he were lucky, no one would miss him for quite some time in this totally confused gathering of humanity. It was a daring plan, but Toby thought a daring plan was in order.

"Where do you think you're going?" Todd asked in a demanding tone.

Toby took his hand off the back door, turned, and greeted his cousin with a scowl.

"I'm going out for some fresh air," Toby replied, harshly. "What does it look like?"

Todd stepped forward and pointed his finger at Toby.

"Why are you wearing your coat and boots?"

"Because it's cold and wet outside, stupid."

"Who you calling stupid?" Todd asked.

Toby approached Todd. They stood nose to nose.

"You. Stupid!" Toby answered.

Todd grabbed Toby by the arm and pulled him to the floor. They fought like two dogs over a scrap of meat. This time, Aunt Lucille wasn't there to stop the resulting scuffle. Toby, for his part, didn't want to fight, but he didn't have a choice. His only alternative was to pin this pain of a cousin before he ruined his plans.

Toby forced Todd's arms to the floor and sat on his stomach.

"Say uncle," Toby ordered.

"No," Todd answered, heroically.

He tried to push Toby off, but Toby was too big and much too strong. But Todd, to his credit, wasn't about to give in easily. Toby had no alternative but to take more drastic actions: He bounced on Todd's stomach until Todd's face turned white as a sheet.

"Say uncle and I'll let you go," Toby said.

Todd belched.

"Uncle," he said.

Toby let go, and Todd rolled to his side, holding his mouth shut with both hands. The freshly eaten meal, complete with milk, cake, and candy, didn't taste nearly as good the second time.

Todd retreated to the dining room, holding his stomach as he cried for sympathy from anyone who would listen. Toby ran from the house, another victory under his belt.

There's nothing colder in winter than the feel of a frozen marble step on a thinly clad posterior. Mother Nature provided the weather; the bank provided the marble step, and Mary provided the rest.

She stared down the street, studying the people she saw in the distance. The crisp air made her eyes water. After several minutes, she thought Toby wouldn't come. She was about to leave, when she saw someone on the next block wearing a red stocking cap and pulling a red sled.

Mary jumped to her feet and ran to meet Toby.

"I didn't think you'd make it," she said.

Toby pulled Old Red to a stop, bent over and took a deep breath.

"I had trouble getting away from the house," he said.

Mary pointed to something on the sled.

"What's that?" she asked.

"That used to be my dog's blanket," Toby answered. "But he got smashed by a car. I took it out of his house. We can use it to cover the crate so no one will see it."

Mary looked at him admiringly.

"You think of everything," she said.

Toby tugged on Old Red's rope.

"We better go."

The road conditions made the trip to St. Andrew Church harder than they had anticipated. Their strides were short. The snow tugged at their feet and stuck to the steel rudders of the sled.

"Do you see him?" Mary asked.

"I see him," Toby replied.

Jimmy Turpin stood at the front window of his house with a jar in one hand and a spoon in the other. He pointed to the road with the spoon and smeared something on the window. A moment later, Billy pushed Jimmy aside, wiped the window with a rag, and pointed to the children.

"Don't stop walking," Toby said. "They're nothing but trouble."

"They scare me," Mary added.

"Jimmy's not as bad as Billy. My dad says he's not all there."

"All there?" Mary asked.

"I think it means he's not very smart. Someone told me Billy was caught taking money out of the poor box in church. I think Daddy made him do it. Daddy made him do a lot of bad things, people say."

"But, Daddy's dead," Mary said.

"But he taught them his ways, but not so good because they keep getting caught."

Mary stopped at the grotto to see the manger and look at the mountain that was to produce so much pain and misery.

"They sure did a lot of work building that manger and choir stand," Mary noted.

Toby turned to her and said, "My dad says there's going to be live animals." Toby pointed to a small clearing. "We'll be watching from over there."

Mary looked at the mountain. It made her feel small and insignificant.

"That big boulder on the top of the cliff looks like an eagle, doesn't it?" she asked.

"More like a buzzard if you ask me," Toby answered. "We better hurry and get this over with."

The church was around the next bend in the road. Mary stopped and turned around.

"What was that?" she said.

"What was what?" Toby asked.

"I thought I heard someone walking on the road behind us."

Toby turned.

"I don't see anyone," he said. "It was probably just some animal running away, maybe a deer. They're all over the place."

When they reached the church, they stood on the steps and stared at the entrance. Mary could still hear the sound of animated voices resonating against the doors. Standing in front of them now, made her feel like a criminal, a thief of the lowest order, when she thought about her reason for being there.

The guilt churned in Mary's stomach like warm milk stirred by a hardy pillow fight at bedtime. When she and

Toby first planned to take the statue, it seemed the right thing to do. Now, she had second doubts.

Toby walked up the steps, firmly planting one foot before lifting the next. The last step taken, he took hold of the door handle and pulled. The door hinges groaned like the painful moan of someone moving an injured joint. Toby stepped back and peeked inside.

Mary scooted behind him and hid her face.

"You don't think God will get us for this, do you?" she asked.

"He's not going to get us," Toby reassured her. "I think He knows what we're doing. And besides, we're not really taking anything. We're only going to move it for a little while, that's all. God will still know where it's at, and He can get it anytime He wants."

"I guess you're right," Mary said. She followed Toby into the church, and then hand-in-hand they walked down the center aisle. Strangely, despite the fear and tension, Mary found this part of the mission somewhat enjoyable. Toby's expression indicated otherwise.

He peered at Mary questioningly; she grinned and turned away.

"What's that over there in the corner?" Mary asked.

Toby released her hand and took several steps forward.

"That's it," Toby said. "That looks like the crate the statue was in. Let's go see."

Toby knelt down to examine it.

"Rats!" he said.

"Toby!" Mary shushed.

She knelt on the floor next to him.

Toby looked at the altar.

"I'm sorry, God." Toby turned to Mary. "The top is nailed shut." Toby scooted the crate around on the floor. "The statue must be inside. It's awful heavy."

Mary put her hand on the box and gave it a shake.

"We have to make sure it's in there," Mary said. "We can't just take it without knowing."

"We need something to pry it open with," Toby said. He reached into his coat pocket and pulled out a double-bladed Case pocket knife. "This ought to do it."

"Where did you get that?" Mary asked.

"My dad gave it to me for my birthday. It's just like his," Toby proudly proclaimed.

He forced the knife blade under the lid and applied slow, steady pressure until the top moved. As he continued, the nails squealed as they were pulled free. The sound echoed throughout the church, giving Mary goose bumps and making her nervous.

"Those nails sure are noisy," she said.

"And there's a lot of them," Toby said, resting.

Mary smiled, her voice was soft. "You can do it," she said.

She touched his arm. Toby ignored her and returned to the job of opening the crate.

"I got it," he said.

Toby lifted the lid and removed the packing material covering the statue. Mary touched the statue's face. It felt warm and almost alive. She expected it to be cold.

"He's beautiful," she said.

Mary picked up the statue and cradled it in her arms like a baby. Toby touched the statue's hand.

"We better get out of here before someone comes in and catches us," he said.

Mary put the statue back into the crate and covered it with the packing material, as if it were a blanket to keep the infant warm. Toby replaced the lid and stepped on the nails to force them back into place.

"You lift that end, and I'll lift this end," he said.

"It's kind of heavy, ain't it," Mary replied.

"It ain't that heavy," Toby said. "All the same, I'm glad I brought Old Red."

They half-stepped down the center aisle to the entrance. Toby stuck his head outside to make sure no one was there.

"The coast is clear," he said.

Toby pushed the door open, and then he and Mary placed the crate on the sled and covered it with the blanket.

Mary looked down the road and said, "Where do you want to go?"

"Old Red's pointing to town. Let's go in that direction."

"What are we going to do when we get there?" Mary asked.

"I don't know," Toby answered. "You got any ideas?"

Toby gave the sled rope a tug and began to walk. Mary helped.

"What about Mt. Carmel Church? No one will be in there until after Christmas."

"I guess we can leave the statue there." Toby looked at the crate. "I just hope we can pull the sled that far."

Mary looked at the blanket-covered crate. It seemed to have grown and put on weight.

"We can do it," Mary said.

She looked at Toby with a half-concealed smile. Her eyes sparkled.

"I told you not to do that," Toby said.

Mary stopped. Something caught her attention.

"What was that?" she asked in a low voice.

"You know," Toby said, "the thing you do with your face."

"No, not that," Mary replied. "Listen." They turned in the direction of the church. "There it is again," she said.

"It's only a dog barking," Toby said.

Agamemnon emerged from behind a tree attached by his teeth to Jimmy's leg. Jimmy yelled, and Billy chased the dog away. Then, he and Jimmy turned to the children.

"Let's get out of here," Toby said.

They pulled the sled as fast as they could, but the sled was heavy, and its sharp steel runners sliced through the snow and dragged on the pavement below.

"The *Turdpins* are gaining on us," Toby huffed, gulping in air.

"That's Turpins," Mary replied, catching her breath.

"We can't outrun them," Toby said. "Follow me." He guided the sled to a row of pines by the grotto. "We better leave Old Red here." He took Mary by the hand, and they ran to the path leading up the side of the mountain. "Do you think you can make it to that ledge?"

Mary looked up. "It's pretty high," she said.

"It's not as high as that tree you had in the backyard of your old house," Toby reminded her, "and you climbed it lots of times."

Mary remembered the tree, but all she could think about at the moment was her dad sitting on the front porch rocking, waiting for her to come home.

"What do you think they want?" Mary asked, climbing.

"I don't know," Toby replied. "But we'll be safe up here."

"What about the statue?" Mary asked, looking back at the sled.

"What about it?" Toby said.

"You said it was valuable. Maybe they'll take it and sell it to someone."

"But it's in the crate," Toby said. "How would they know what's inside?"

"Maybe they don't care what inside," Mary said. "It's just something for them to steal."

Mary and Toby stood on the ledge and looked down at the Turpin brothers. Agamemnon poked his head out of some bushes and barked. Billy threw a snowball at him, but his aim was bad, and his snowball poorly made. Toby, in turn, threw a snowball at Billy, hitting him in the head. Then, the war began.

No one struck a mortal blow, even though countless snowballs were hurled, and Toby hit his target on almost every throw.

During the battle, a car drove past. Mary tugged Toby's arm.

"That looked like Sheriff Durben's patrol car," Mary said.

"He can't help us now," Toby replied. "We're thieves, remember."

Billy ran to the road. When Sheriff Durben's patrol car was out of sight, he yelled for Jimmy to get the crate.

"You leave that alone!" Toby shouted.

But the Turpins ignored him and ran away.

Toby and Mary came down from the ledge and sat on Old Red. Toby made a snowball and threw it at a tree. It hit with a plop, spattering on the bark like mud.

"They took the statue, and we're to blame," he said.

"We couldn't stop them," Mary replied. "They were too big."

"And we were too dumb," Toby muttered. He looked at Mary. "Where's your star?" he asked.

Mary felt her lapel. It wasn't there. She stood to see if it had fallen on the ground.

"I must have lost it when we were running," she said.

"If you want, we can go back and look for it," Toby said.

"No, it's getting late, and we'll never find it in all that snow." Her voice quivered. "It's lost forever."

"I'm sorry," Toby said. "I should have thought of a better plan."

"It's not your fault," Mary said. "What do you want to do?"

"I don't know," Toby answered. "We can't go to Sheriff Durben. We stole the statue first. He'll just put us in jail."

"Jail?" Mary said.

"Probably," Toby replied.

"There has to be something we can do," Mary said.

Toby stood and brushed himself off. His face had an expression Mary had never before seen, one of resolve.

"Let's follow the Turpins," Toby boldly declared, "and see where they take *our* statue."

"That's *Turdpins*," Mary replied.

# Chapter XXIV

Jimmy waddled from side to side as he carried the crate down the snow-packed road. Their house was next to Daddy's Texaco station. It all belonged to the boys now, but they rented the filling station to Daddy's old mechanic. Work was not a word in the boy's vocabulary, although searching car upholstery for loose coins and whatnots apparently didn't fall under that category.

When they arrived home, they could hardly wait to open the crate and count the money. Jimmy stood by the front door and held the crate while Billy searched his pocket for the keys. The door was barred and had two padlocks. He considered most of the people in town dishonest, and so never left the house unsecured. As for money and valuables, anything he had of value was safely tucked away in the overstuffed, dirty clothes hamper, the last place he thought anyone would look.

"Do you think the kids will snitch on us?" Jimmy asked.

"And get their parents in trouble? Who do you think stole this money?" Billy opened the door and pulled Jimmy inside. "Put the crate on the kitchen table so I can open it."

Jimmy did as instructed, and then retrieved his peanut butter jar and spoon and began to eat. Billy got a knife from the cabinet and pried the crate open.

Jimmy pointed at the crate with the spoon.

"What's that?" he asked.

"It's a statue," Billy said in disbelief. "What do you think it is?"

Billy slapped his hand on the table.

Jimmy jumped back.

"I thought you said the bank money was inside?"

Jimmy stepped forward to get a closer look. He scratched his head with the peanut butter spoon as he examined the contents of the crate. Billy's anger exploded. He grabbed Jimmy by the back of the neck and shoved Jimmy's head nearer the crate.

"See! There ain't no money!" Billy yelled. "Are you blind?"

Billy imagined Sheriff Durben coming through the front door any minute, asking questions he didn't want to answer. He wanted to run and hide, but he had no place to go.

"It's a pretty statue," Jimmy said.

Jimmy anchored the spoon in his mouth, touched the statue's arm, and smiled.

"It's a pretty mess those kids got us into," Billy replied.

"Can we keep it?" Jimmy asked.

"No, we can't keep it," Billy answered. "We got to get rid of it."

He picked up the statue. His arms trembled as he lifted it over his head.

Jimmy covered his ears. "Don't," he cried.

Billy lowered his arms. "I ain't going to jail over no statue," he said, putting the statue back into the crate. "I got to figure something out."

Billy walked around the kitchen table, talking to himself as Jimmy watched and kept count of the revolutions. It had been a long time since Billy's last idea, so when one finally formed in his brain it wasn't immediately recognized.

"I got it," he said. "We'll leave the statue at Mt. Carmel Church. No one is there at this time of the day. The preacher there is a friend of Reverend Richmann's and is sure to give it back to him."

"But how would he know?" Jimmy asked.

"Preachers know these things," Billy replied. "They talk to each other all the time about statues and such."

"But, it's at the other end of town," Jimmy moaned.

"Then, we better hurry, cause I ain't getting caught with this statue, and I ain't going anywhere near St. Andrew's."

Jimmy carried the crate outside and put it on the truck bed while Billy started the motor. The motor backfired, blew a cloud of black smoke from the exhaust pipe, and started with a rumble that shook the entire truck.

"Don't drive too fast," Jimmy insisted. "The road's real slick."

"I know the road's slick, you idiot," Billy replied. "We were just walking on it." He slapped Jimmy on the side. "I'll do the driving, you watch out for the sheriff."

Billy was reluctant to drive even in good weather. He had had several wrecks, mostly running into trees and road signs that refused to get out of his way. He and Jimmy ended up in the hospital on more than one occasion. Billy really would have preferred to walk, which was about as fast as he drove. When they arrived at the church, Billy ordered Jimmy to go inside to see if anyone was there, praying or some-thing. As usual, Jimmy wanted Billy to come along. Not that he was afraid of the church, only the aloneness he felt inside.

Mary and Toby watched from the side of a nearby building.

Mary whispered into Toby's ear, "What do you think they're up to?"

"I don't know," Toby said, rubbing the side of his face.

A car drove by--the children turned to see who it was.

"Wasn't that your dad?" Mary asked.

"That was my dad, all right. I forgot that he was supposed to pick up the statue at St. Andrew Church and take it over to the manger. I think he's going to be really mad when he gets there."

"I should have been home by now," Mary said.

"Me too," Toby answered.

"There they go," Mary said.

Billy and Jimmy got into the truck. The truck backfired, and the Turpins drove away.

"Let's see if they really left the statue inside the church or an empty crate," Toby said. "It could be some kind of a trick."

Toby pulled his sled over to the church. He stood at the bottom of the steps and looked at the door. Mary stepped forward.

"You go in first," Toby said. "I've never been in there before."

"All right, but you follow me real close."

Mary opened the door. The church was darker than St. Andrew Church, which had an abundance of stained glass windows. It was smaller, too. Something she had never previously noticed. She assumed that churches were all the same except, of course, for their church, which was really a hall.

Mary took a step to the left; Toby took a step to the right. The floor creaked, and they stopped.

"Do you see the crate?" Mary asked.

"No," Toby replied. "Why don't you go over to that row of chairs in the front and see if it's there. I'll look around back here."

Mary tiptoed down the center aisle, checking the pews as she went along, but all she saw were a few hymnals and a forgotten handkerchief or two. When she arrived at the altar, she paused long enough to say a little prayer before continuing her search. Toby was in the back moving aside some cardboard boxes stacked in a corner.

Mary saw something in the shadows and walked over to it. "I found it!" she said. Her voice was excited.

She placed her hands over her mouth, but it was too late. Toby bolted like a colt at the sound of thunder, knocking over several of the boxes.

"Shhhhh!" he hushed. "Someone might hear you."

Toby went over to the front door and looked outside. When he was certain it was clear, he rushed over to Mary. She was on her knees next to the crate. Toby knelt by her side, took out his pocket knife and removed the crate's lid.

"It's the statue," he said.

"What are we going to do now?" Mary asked.

Mary touched the statue with the tips of her fingers and smiled.

"Nothing," Toby replied. "This is where we wanted to bring it, isn't it?"

Mary shrugged. "But suppose they come back, or suppose they tell Pastor Amos, and he takes it back in time for the service?"

"Then, we better hide it," Toby huffed.

"Hide it where?" Mary asked.

"How about someplace in here?" he said. "I don't think we have time to go anywhere else." Toby turned in a circle and surveyed the area. "How about behind that?" Toby said, pointing to the organ. "No one will ever see it there."

"That ought to work," Mary said. "If someone does come looking for it, they'll think it was taken somewhere else."

Toby sealed the crate, and Mary helped him move it.

"We better get out of here," Toby said.

Mary slipped her hand into Toby's. He didn't realize that he held something warm and soft until he was outside. When he did, he immediately escaped her clutches and reached for the sled rope.

# Chapter XXV

The parsonage door had a small, stained glass window, in the center of which was a cherub holding a candle with a bright yellow flame. It was a cordial looking angel, or so Jeffrey thought, and it seemed to invite the guest inside. Jeffrey asked himself why he had never noticed the angel before. He had been there often enough, but, as always, he was in a rush to go somewhere else.

He tapped his shoes on the porch to remove the snow and ice, and knocked on the door. The reverend's wife answered. He greeted her with a smile.

"Good afternoon, Mrs. Richmann," Jeffrey said. "Is your husband in? I'm here to take the statue over to the manger."

"Come in out of the cold," she replied, "and I'll get him for you. In the meantime, make yourself at home in the study."

Jeffrey envied the reverend's study and admired his collection of books, but, even more, he yearned to have the time to read them. They contained a world he was eager to explore, a world without numbers, ledgers, and balance sheets. He had often thought about borrowing one or two, but he never got around to it.

"Hello, Jeffrey," Reverend Richmann said. "You're early, but I left the church door open for you. The statue is in the crate next to the altar."

"I just came from the church, but I didn't see the crate."

"That's strange. Oh, well," Reverend Richmann said with a shrug. "I guess I'll have to show you where I put it. How about a cup of coffee before we leave?"

"It'll have to be a quick cup," Jeffrey said. "I have a house full of relatives. I'm afraid it's my year to be tormented."

He sat down on the couch and fingered through a book that was lying open on the coffee table.

"Did you see the lanterns at the grotto?" Reverend Richmann asked. "I think you'll be able to see the light from anywhere in town."

"Probably from anywhere in the next county," Jeffrey joked, "judging from the number I saw."

"We'll start the generator as soon as the sun goes down," Reverend Richmann said. "The choir will arrive a little earlier to practice."

"It looks like everything's going as planned."

"Here's the coffee," the reverend said.

They toasted success with the clicking of their coffee cups, drank without discussing any topics of interest or chit-chat to pass the time, and then went over to the church.

"I know I put the statue right here," Reverend Richmann said, pointing. He scratched his head in disbelief, and then walked around the altar, searching for the elusive crate. "You don't suppose someone moved it, do you?"

"Why would anyone do that?" Jeffrey asked. An image of the choir leader invaded his thoughts. "Let's drive over to the manger and see if it's there. We can use my car; it's still warm."

Jeffrey felt something was wrong, but he kept his fears to himself as he drove to the manger.

"You better go to the manger alone," Reverend Richmann said. He looked up at the grotto. "My legs aren't what they used to be."

"My pleasure. I'll be back in a minute."

Jeffrey ran to the manger and returned a short time later. He stood by the car door, held his side and forced the cold air in and out of his aching lungs. Reverend Richmann rolled down the window.

"Is it there?" he asked.

Jeffrey shook his head no and puffed out the words, "I checked the entire area and didn't see it anywhere."

"Let's go back and look in the sacristy," Reverend Richmann said. "I pray I put it there in my haste to get ready for the Christmas Eve service. Sometimes I think my mind is failing me."

The reverend's face reflected his distress.

"Nonsense," Jeffrey replied. "You're as sharp as the day we first met. If you say it was there, it was there. Let's go back and look again."

They searched the entire church from basement to attic and the parsonage as well. The reverend's wife was even recruited in the effort. But in the confusion, she made the mistake of letting the cat out of the bag when the choir director telephoned during the hunt. Five minutes later, the telephone rang, and kept ringing. It seemed that everyone in the congregation wanted to know what happened to the statue.

Reverend Richmann called the sheriff and sat on the couch with his wife to wait his arrival. Jeffrey did all he could to comfort them before going home to face the music orchestrating there.

Jeffrey entered the house and discovered another mystery was unfolding--Where was Toby? Todd was more than willing to fill him in on all the sordid details, and this time Jeffrey gave his complaints serious consideration. After Todd told his story, Jeffrey walked outside to look for Toby. The first place he went was the garage to see if Old Red was gone. Jeffrey told himself that Toby probably decided to go sledding on the hill after his run-in with his cousin.

Jeffrey kissed Marge good-bye and made his excuses to the guests before departing, but when he arrived at the hill, it was vacant. The weary oak rested in solitude as a cold northern breeze caressed its wounds.

Jeffrey paced in front of his car. He asked himself where to go next, when all of a sudden he saw Cynthia walking in the distance, carrying what appeared to be a large cooking pot.

"Cynthia! Cynthia Klein!" Jeffrey shouted.

Jeffrey waved. Cynthia turned, took a step back, and stood on the sidewalk and watched as he got into his car and drove over.

"Good day, Mrs. Klein."

"Good day, Mr. Carston." Cynthia answered with a slight hesitation. She stepped closer to the car. "Is something wrong?" she asked, adding before Jeffrey could answer. "Because if it's about the loan payment, I know I'm late, but I'll make two payments next month. I promise. It's Christmas, and I guess I spent too much."

"Loan?" he answered. "No, no," he said with a grin. "I better start over, and please call me Jeffrey." He paused. "I'm looking for my son Toby. Have you by any chance seen him today?"

Cynthia took a quick breath and smiled in a somber fashion.

"No, I haven't seen him...Jeffrey. But I can ask Mary as soon as I get home from delivering this soup to the hall."

"In that case, how about a ride?" Jeffrey asked. "I'm getting a little worried, and Mary might be able to help."

"I wouldn't want to put you out," she replied.

"On the contrary, I'm putting you in," he said, smiling. "In my car, that is."

"Well, if you insist."

"I do insist. It's much too cold for you to be out walking in the snow with a heavy soup pot."

Jeffrey drove Cynthia to the hall to deliver the soup, and then headed for her house. On the way, they discussed the joys and tribulations of parenting. Jeffrey discovered they had a lot in common and remembered that at one time in the not-too-distant past he knew that.

"There they are," Cynthia said.

She pointed down one of the side streets. Jeffrey turned the steering wheel.

"What do you think those two have been up to?" Jeffrey asked.

His voice held a sigh of relief, but his curiosity was apparent.

"I'm afraid to think of the possibilities," Cynthia replied, "but at least they're safe."

"I can't wait to hear what Toby has to say," Jeffrey said. "He's real good at providing explanations."

Jeffrey hit the brakes. The car slid to a stop in the slush. The children jumped back, their eyes were as big as saucers. A pretentiously angry Jeffrey got out of the car, walked over to them and immediately directed them to the rear door of the car, pointing the way with an extended arm and stiff index finger.

"You two get in the back seat while I put the sled in the trunk," he said, harshly.

The children did as instructed, wide-eyed and speechless.

Cynthia turned her head around like an owl's so Mary could see her face when she entered the car.

"I thought we had a deal?" Cynthia said. She looked at Mary as if she were as transparent as water. "I can't believe you did this."

"But, Mom," Mary said, looking at Toby from the corners of her eyes.

"But Mom nothing, young lady," Cynthia replied. She shook her finger at her daughter and turned around. "You wait till I get you home!"

Jeffrey got into the car and glared at Toby.

"What do you have to say for yourself, young man?"

Toby looked at the floor.

"I'm sorry, Dad. I should have told you I was going out with Old Red."

"Yes, you should have." Jeffrey said. He started the car. "You're just lucky I have a bigger problem at the moment to deal with, or you'd really be in the dog house."

The two children sank deep into the seat, the size of their guilt measured by the depth of the hole into which they sank. Cynthia and Jeffrey turned to each other for reassurance and comfort, their distress measured by the size of their troubled hearts.

The car contained an uneasy silence as Jeffrey drove Cynthia and Mary home. When the car came to a stop, the silence continued. Mary and Toby held their breaths.

Cynthia looked at her hands, her face flushed.

"I want to thank you for the ride," she said, "and apologize for any inconvenience Mary may have caused."

Jeffrey answered with a courteous nod, "It is I who should be thanking you."

Cynthia stepped out of the car and walked over to the sidewalk. Mary gave Toby a quick glance, got out of the car, and walked over to her mother, where she quietly waited for the scolding to commence. Cynthia was about to begin the lecture, when Jeffrey rolled down the window to speak.

"I just want to say that if you need anything in the future, please give me a call or come pay me a visit at the bank." Jeffrey paused. "And before I forget, apparently I made a bookkeeping error, one of many mistakes, I fear. Your loan is paid in full. Good-bye and Merry Christmas," he said, driving away.

Chapter XXVI

Sheriff Durben was at the parsonage questioning Reverend Richmann and writing his report. It wasn't an easy job. The parsonage was filled with members of the congregation wanting information, all at the same time. When the report was finished, Sheriff Durben and Reverend Richmann went over to the church. It wasn't any better there.

The church was filled with people complaining, arguing, or looking in, under, over, and around anything that didn't move out of the way. More than one voice spoke suspiciously of Jeffrey. The comments, however, were immediately quelled by either Reverend Richmann or Pastor Amos, who had arrived to console his friend and help out if he could.

It was a mystery. No one could offer an explanation other than theft. It shocked everyone to think that this could happen in Mayfield. Word of the loathsome deed spread through town as fast as the common cold. With the blessing of the first sneeze, it seemed everyone had a theory.

Sheriff Durben started the investigation in the usual manner: First, get the facts; next, go carefully over the facts and resolve any unanswered or ambiguous issues; finally, question the most likely suspects, to include the short list of petty thieves and near-do-wells living in town. He started with the Turpin brothers. Their place was close to the scene of the crime, and Billy had been in and out of trouble most of his life, to include the theft of money from St. Andrew Church.

When Sheriff Durben arrived at their house, he saw Billy at the window watching him, but as soon as the sheriff got out of the patrol car, Billy disappeared. Sheriff Durben would have preferred to light a fresh cigar and make the Turpins sweat for a few minutes, but he didn't have the time, and he wasn't in the mood to play. Instead, he walked over to the truck, looked it over, then proceeded to the house in a measured pace.

He stomped on the porch, made a fist, and was about to bang on the front door when it opened.

A smiling face emerged from the gloom inside and greeted the sheriff. "Come in, Sheriff Durben. What can we do for you?" Billy said.

The sheriff pushed him aside and entered. Jimmy sat on a chair by the radio; he looked constipated. Billy remained at the door, his mouth still supporting a larger than life smile.

Sheriff Durben turned to Billy and growled the words, "You can turn it over right now and make this easy on the both of us. Just tell me where it's at?"

"Where what's at?" Billy asked. "Me and Jimmy have been here all day, not bothering nobody."

"If you've been here all day *not bothering nobody*, why is the hood of your truck hot? I don't see any heat wave outside." The sheriff stepped closer to Billy. "And how did you know it happened today?"

"Oh, the truck. I forgot," Billy said with a sly grin. "Me and Jimmy took a box we found today by the side of the road over to Mt. Carmel Church. I didn't know we were doing anything wrong. We thought it must have fallen off a delivery van or something."

The sheriff was fully aware that Billy wasn't going to tell him the truth, but he was unable to prove otherwise at the moment.

"Why did you take it to Mt. Carmel Church?"

"Because it had a statue in it, a holy statue." Billy looked at Jimmy. Jimmy nodded his agreement, and Billy walked over to the kitchen table. "We didn't know what else to do with it. We couldn't just leave it there. It wouldn't be Christian-like."

"Why Mt. Carmel Church?" Sheriff Durben asked. He walked over to Billy and spoke directly into his face. "Why there? St. Andrew Church is just down the road."

"Me and Reverend Richmann don't get along so well, and Jimmy wanted to see the lights and decorations in town. Maybe stop by the hall and see what they're planning for tonight."

"I like the lights," Jimmy mumbled. "They look real pretty, especially the red ones, and the hall always has good food at Christmas time."

Billy walked over to Jimmy and placed his hand on his brother's shoulder. The sheriff circled his quarry. After the second pass, he stood in front of Billy and spoke. "So, you two are nothing more than two good Samaritans. Aren't you?"

Jimmy looked confused.

Billy spoke out. "We ain't one of them," he said. "We're telling you the truth." He looked at Jimmy. "Ain't we?"

Jimmy lowered his head and said, "We found it by the road just like Billy said."

The sheriff took a deep breath. "Where's your telephone?" he asked, angrily. "I have to call Reverend Richmann and have him meet us at Mt. Carmel Church."

"Us?" Billy asked.

"Yes, us. You two are coming with me." Sheriff Durben said. "Where's the phone?"

Billy pointed to the front door.

"The phone's outside in the booth," he said.

Sheriff Durben walked over to Billy.

"You got a nickel?"

Billy dug deep into his pocket until he found a nickel. The sheriff took it, carefully inspected it, and then left for the phone booth. Billy and Jimmy stood at the window and watched as the sheriff spoke to Reverend Richmann. The sheriff kept his attention focused on the two faces peering at him. When he was finished giving Reverend Richmann the good news, he went back to the house.

"Get your coats on," the sheriff said in a commanding tone.

"Why do we have to go?" Billy asked, sheepishly. "I told you where the statue is."

"Because I said so, and because I want to keep an eye on you until I get this all straightened out. Now, get ready."

It looked like a Fourth of July parade as the onslaught of cars and trucks drove in single file down the street to Mt. Carmel Church, Pastor Amos' car in the lead.

The sheriff and the Turpin brothers were parked at the church, waiting in the patrol car when the flood of sheet metal approached.

Sheriff Durben turned to his suspects. He had a crooked smile.

"You boys better be right," the sheriff said. "I smell a lynching."

"It's inside, honest," Billy insisted. "We're not lying."

"It better be," the sheriff said.

Billy trembled, his face paled as he and the sheriff entered the church. Jimmy remained in the car. Neither man nor peanut butter spoon could pry him from his seat.

"Well, where is it?" Sheriff Durben asked in an aggravated tone.

The sheriff crossed his arms and waited for an answer. Billy looked lost and bewildered. The number of people inside the church increased with each passing second. They circled Billy and mumbled their displeasure.

"We put it right over there," Billy said, scratching his head. He walked over and pointed to the spot on the floor where he and Jimmy had left the statue. "Right here, honest!"

"Perhaps someone moved it, again," the sheriff said.

"I think he's just plain lying," someone replied.

Someone bumped into Billy and said, "I'll get the truth out of him."

Billy moved behind the sheriff.

"There'll be none of that here," Sheriff Durben advised.

Pastor Amos turned to Reverend Richmann and said, "I have a suggestion, James. Why don't we make this a joint celebration this year? Something tells me it was meant to be, and," he said with a chuckle, "there's plenty of room at the inn."

Reverend Richmann looked at the people, smiled, and nodded his approval. He raised his arms and clapped his hands.

"Your attention please," he said. "We're going to hold our services together this year. I'm sure the statue will eventually be found. In the meantime, let's make the best of the situation and join our friends at the hall. I want everyone to spread the word." Pastor Amos whispered something to Reverend Richmann. Reverend Richmann nodded his approval and smiled. "And please tell everyone to bring some covered dishes, especially dessert. There's going to be a lot of hungry people there," adding for the sheriff and Pastor Amos' ears, "I've got a good feeling about this."

Sheriff Durben had his doubts. He was in a bad mood and was determined to stay that way until things started to make sense. To make matters worse, he had a handful of Turpins, but had nothing to charge them with. He told Billy to get his brother and go home before he changed his mind and went to fetch a rope.

# Chapter XXVII

"Get out of here, you filthy rodent!" Rosey yelled.

"Don't run him my way," Honeycut cried.

A rat jumped out of an empty dynamite box. Rosey threw a shovel at it to hurry its departure. Honeycut danced a jig until the rat crawled under some old timbers. Rosey laughed and packed the remaining explosives into the holes the workers had previously drilled through the rock and rubble.

"What do you think?" Honeycut asked.

"I've seen bigger rats," Rosey said, inspecting his work.

"Not the rat, the explosives."

"Forget about the explosives," Rosey said, "and the rats. I'm done."

"What are you all riled about?" Honeycut asked. He grabbed the shovel Rosey had thrown at the wayward rodent and propped it against the wall. "The engineers say there's nothing to worry about. If it's good enough for them, it's good enough for yours truly."

"I know what the engineers said," Rosey answered. He kicked the dynamite box aside. "I'll bet they all got an A+ in every one of those fancy classes they took at those expensive schools out East. All for the purpose of telling me a book knows more than I do about this or that."

Honeycut shrugged. "Well, I put my money on Jerry." Honeycut crossed his arms in a show of confidence. "As long as he's singing, I'm happy."

"I don't trust any animal that can't make proper sounds," Rosey replied. "Especially a canary that can't sing."

"You got that right," Honeycut said with a laugh. "I never thought I'd see the day a canary needed a *tater* sack to carry a tune. Seems to me the only time he sings anymore is when someone feeds him, but that still doesn't explain why you're so flustered."

"I've got a funny feeling that something's wrong." Rosey adjusted the lamp attached to his hard hat. "You know, like when a rabbit runs over your grave."

"Is that one of those Polish things?" Honeycut asked.

"Depends on the rabbit."

Rosey knelt on the ground and laced the dynamite fuses together. Honeycut was anxious to leave. He kept turning around as if listening for something. This time it was Steven's footsteps he heard.

"What's keeping you?" Steven asked. "It's nearly six o'clock."

Honeycut looked at his watch and stepped aside to make room for Steven.

"We're ready," Rosey answered. "Except for Honeycut who keeps not hearing something."

"And I still ain't hearing it," Honeycut said, looking down the shaft.

Rosey lit the fuses and took Honeycut by the arm.

"Let's go," Rosey said.

Honeycut yelled at the top of his lungs, "Fire in the hole!"

It startled both Rosey and Steven.

"What in heaven's name was that all about?" Steven asked.

"Nothing," Honeycut replied. "I just always wanted to yell that."

Steven shook his head and walked away. Rosey followed. Honeycut took the lead.

The fuse burned along the ground with intermittent spits and sputters. Each inch of fuse counted off the seconds.

"I haven't heard Jerry singing today," Honeycut said.

"Of course you haven't," Steven replied. He stopped momentarily to kick a lump of coal out of his way. "Jerry died last night."

"He *what* last night?" Rosey asked. He turned to Steven. "Why wasn't I informed?"

"You were informed," Steven insisted. "Don't you read the bulletin board?"

"I don't always have time to read every item on the bulletin board before a shift."

"Well, don't worry." Steven said. "The engineers and I conducted a thorough investigation of the shafts. Nothing was found and nothing was left to chance. We think it was Jerry's time to turn in his whistle. He was at least four years old, maybe five," Steven said.

Steven appeared unconcerned, but Rosey and Honeycut looked at each other and shuddered.

"I just felt one of those rabbits," Honeycut said.

"Four years, maybe five," Rosey said aloud to himself. "I wonder how old that is in people years?"

"What?" Steven asked.

"Nothing," Rosey replied. "Let's get out of here."

A rail car was a few feet ahead. It was Rosey's original intent to stop there and wait for the explosion to occur, but not anymore. No one had to say a word. They hopped into the rail car and headed for the surface.

Honeycut put his watch to his ear and said, "I never realized how slow these cars were."

The rail car hit some rough spots in the track. Honeycut adjusted the lamp on his hard hat. Steven jerked forward. Rosey's face wrenched with anger.

Honeycut held his wristwatch in front of his eyes, gave the minute hand a solemn stare, looked down the mine shaft, and blurted out, "It's going to blow any second now."

Rosey kicked Honeycut's foot.

"Did Santa bring you a brand new watch for Christmas?"

"Calm down, Rosey," Steven said.

The rail car stopped well short of the mine entrance because of some repair work being done on the tracks. Steven and Honeycut jumped out and ran for the exit. Rosey sat like a bump on a log, brooding.

"Come on, Rosey," Steven yelled. "We have to get out of here."

"I'll come in my own good time," Rosey replied.

⁓

Steven and Honeycut stood in the safety of the control shack and stared at the mine entrance from the window. They didn't utter a word or move a muscle until the explosion was heard.

A split second later the mine belched a cloud of pitch-black smoke that formed a giant mushroom as it headed skyward. The blast was far more powerful than they expected.

"There had to be a gas pocket down there," Steven said.

"Gas and coal dust make a deadly combination," Honeycut answered, shaking his head."

"Rosey!" Steven yelled.

They ran to the mine entrance as fast as their legs would carry them. The smoke and coal dust formed a thick black cloud that stretched across the entrance like a curtain. Honeycut called for Rosey. Steven was about to go in when Rosey emerged, covered with soot from head to toe.

"I guess Jerry knew more than the engineers after all," Steven said, laughing.

A tear ran down his face as he tried to control his laughter. Rosey had the appearance of a burnt china doll. His hair was frizzled where it stuck out from under his hard hat. His clothing was charred, and his eyes looked like two marsh-mallows floating in a bowl of chocolate pudding.

"What are you two laughing at?" Rosey asked.

"Nothing," Honeycut answered, putting his hand over his mouth.

Steven turned away, pretending to cough.

"Why today of all days?" Rosey moaned.

He brushed himself off, grumbled and complained about the training of engineers and the lifespan of canaries. Paul arrived just as they were going into the shower room. A slight grin appeared on his face when he saw Rosey, but he made no comment on the apparent apparition standing before him.

Steven asked Paul why he was there. Paul told him that he was at the community center, when he felt the rumble from the explosion. Everyone there expected it. Nevertheless, he wanted to make sure everything was all right. Steven reassured him that everything was fine; even though he wouldn't have the luxury of working shaft number four anytime in the near future. After Christmas, they would evaluate the damage and go on from there. Nothing else could be done at the moment. He shrugged it off as a lesson learned and vowed to buy another canary as soon as possible.

Paul insisted on checking Rosey's condition, but Rosey was in no mood for a physical. Steven, however, was concerned and wasn't about to let Rosey leave without Paul's okay. Rosey complained all the louder, but finally allowed Paul to treat his burns and nothing more.

After Paul finished treating Rosey's burns he gave him some medication to take home along with some instructions for its use, then he drove back to the hall to tell the people what had happened.

Steven sat on one of the benches positioned in front of a row of metal lockers and thought about his prospects for the future.

Rosey stared into the locker room mirror.

"My face is as red as a beet," Rosey said. "And that white cream Doc spread on it like butter on toast makes it look even worse." Rosey walked over to Honeycut; Honeycut took a step back. "What time do you have on that brand new watch of yours?"

"*Pert* near quarter past seven," Honeycut said with a grin.

"Quarter past seven!" Rosey yelled. He went back over to the mirror and once again examined his face. "I'm late, and I'm redder than Santa's britches." Rosey forced a smile and turned to Honeycut. Honeycut braced himself for the worse. "Honeycut, old friend, I need you to do me a favor."

# Chapter XXVIII

When Paul returned to the hall, Flo was waiting for him at the door. Food was being served, and the walls echoed the clattering of steel utensils scraping china plates. She took him by the hand and escorted him to a pair of empty chairs at the table where Pastor Amos sat.

The pastor's face was aglow with pride as he gently clutched a small box to his chest. Paul knew what was inside--blue booties. The reverend's wife once joked that her husband wouldn't allow pink for the first born since he had a direct line to the Almighty. Paul grinned and thought about his own wedding arrangements. Flo wanted the ceremony in June, and so did he. Their only disagreement was the year and the size of the resulting family.

"Are you all right?" Flo asked. "You have that distant look."

Paul shook his head. "Just thinking."

"Sometimes I think you think too much," Flo replied. The front door swung open. Flo turned. "Look who just came in."

Sheriff Durben's face was pale. He signaled to Paul and Jeffrey, and then went back outside. They followed without an explanation. It was curious behavior even for the sheriff.

"What's this all about, Sheriff?" Paul asked.

"Get in the patrol car," the sheriff answered. "I'm not saying a word until we get there."

"Get where?" Jeffrey asked.

Sheriff Durben gave him a blank stare. "Just get in."

They drove straight out of town and stopped at the grotto. A landslide had covered the road with a mountain of dirt and rock. The manger and choir stand had been completely destroyed and lay scattered in bits and pieces among the debris.

"I was on my way back to town when it happened," Sheriff Durben explained. He stepped out of the car with his flashlight and walked over to the edge of the landslide. Jeffrey and Paul followed. The sheriff was visibly shaken by the event. His voice betrayed his emotions. "The whole mountain shook just as I drove by. I couldn't believe what I was seeing in my rear view mirror."

"It's a nightmare," Jeffrey said. "We could have all been killed."

"We're lucky the service was cancelled," Paul said.

"We're luckier than that," Sheriff Durben informed them. "Come with me." He spoke with a commanding arm gesture, waving the flashlight in the air like a baton. "The cave's been reopened, and there's something inside you need to see "

They entered the cave. It was dark and damp and smelled of flesh turned to dust. Sheriff Durben switched on his flashlight and focused it on the skeleton of a man lying on the ground near the entrance. He had gold teeth, a tattered red bandana, and was holding a rusty revolver in his bony fingers. Next to him on a large flat rock situated above the ground like a table, was a pair of handcuffs and two stuffed moneybags from the savings and loan.

"You know what this means," Paul said.

"It means we've all been fools," Jeffrey replied.

Sheriff Durben turned and said matter-of-factly as he left, "It only means we've made mistakes, nothing more."

"What now?" Paul asked.

"Take me to the bank," Jeffrey insisted.

The drive gave everyone time to think about what had happened, and what they had seen. When they entered Jeffrey's office, Jeffrey went straight to the phone and called the Governor at home. Sheriff Durben and Paul went over to the window. Sheriff Durben saw a man sitting on the bench in front of the bus station. The man was looking at a silver-colored object he had taken from some kind of a sack.

"Excuse me, Paul," Sheriff Durben said. "I need to talk to that man on the bench."

"Go ahead," Paul said, turning to Jeffrey. "He's going to be awhile."

Sheriff Durben approached the man sitting on the bench and took note of everything about him--the army issued overcoat, the boots, the stocking cap, and the tote sack lying next to him on the bench.

The man said and did nothing when the sheriff stood in front of him. In fact, the man seemed to be daydreaming.

"Is your name Captain David Angelo?" Sheriff Durben asked.

The man was surprised to hear his name. He looked up and pulled his tote sack closer to his side. Sheriff Durben felt the bump on his head.

"Yes, I'm Captain David Angelo."

He held out his hand. Sheriff Durben paused, and then shook it.

Angelo asked, "Is something wrong?"

"I'm afraid there is." Sheriff Durben pointed to the bus schedule posted on the bus station door. "That schedule is incorrect. The bus won't be coming. The road is out, and I expect it will remain out for the next couple of days."

Captain Angelo didn't seem upset by the news.

"I thought as much," he replied.

"Where's your home?" Sheriff Durben asked.

"Paradise," he answered.

"Paradise?" the sheriff asked.

"Paradise, Montana." Captain Angelo looked at the sky and took a deep breath. "As soon as I can get a bus ticket, that's my next and hopefully last stop."

The sheriff pointed down the street and said, "See that white, two-story building?"

Angelo turned. "Yes."

"It's a boarding house. You can spend the next couple of days there."

Angelo put his hand in his pocket and pulled out a few wrinkled dollar bills. "I'm afraid I'm going to have to make other arrangements if I want to go home."

"You can't do that. I don't allow loitering in Mayfield," the sheriff replied. "Just tell the desk clerk that Sheriff Durben sent you. The county will foot the bill."

The sheriff turned to leave, then stopped and took something out of his pocket.

"This isn't yours by any chance?" he asked.

Angelo's eyes widened.

"It looks like my wallet, at least the one I used to own." Sheriff Durben handed it to him, and he opened it. His eyes teared. "She looked prettier in life, my Eloise," Angelo said. "She's been gone too long, and I even longer." Angelo looked up. "Thank you, Sheriff."

The sheriff reached into his pocket and pulled out a five-dollar bill.

"There was some money in the wallet, but the bills were in bad shape. I'll turn them into the bank later and get repaid. If you're hungry, there's food at the hall. It's usually good, if you don't mind a little preaching with the dessert. The hall's a few blocks in that direction." The sheriff smiled and pointed the way. "Everyone's welcome. But if you don't want to go in, just knock on the back door and the ladies will serve you there. And don't worry about the bus ticket.

There'll be one waiting for you at the boarding house. As I said, I don't allow loitering in Mayfield."

Sheriff Durben waived good-bye and walked away.

Angelo stood and called out to him. "Why are you helping me?"

Sheriff Durben turned and said with a rare smile, "Merry Christmas, Captain Angelo."

~~∽ ∼~~

"Are you two ready to go?" the sheriff asked, entering the office.

"Anytime he is," Paul said, turning to Jeffrey.

Jeffrey was at his desk making some notes in a ledger.

"I'll be finished in a minute," he answered. "I put everything we recovered into the vault and took a quick inventory, but I have one more job to take care of before we leave."

"Don't you ever quit working?" Sheriff Durben asked.

"This isn't work. It's restitution."

Jeffrey signed some papers, placed them in an envelope, and tucked it away in his suit coat pocket. Leaning back in his chair, he stared at his father's portrait.

"What's wrong?" Paul asked.

"Things could have been different, *should* have been different," Jeffrey replied.

"What's done is done," Sheriff Durben said. "Let's go."

Sheriff Durben drove to the hall and parked in front of the door.

"You two go ahead," he said.

"See you inside," Paul replied.

The sheriff sat behind the wheel with his eyes closed. After a minute of thought, he rolled down the window and retrieved a cigar from the glove compartment.

"I should have reopened that cave," Sheriff Durben said aloud. "I should have checked it out. Why didn't I see it?"

He bit off the tip of his cigar, spat it out the window, and cursed himself for botching the investigation. The more he thought about it, the angrier he became until his eyes glazed over and his anger exploded. He pounded his fist against the dash. The pain relieved the guilt, but only for a second. He swore that he would never make that mistake again.

He got a match from his pocket, but before he could light his cigar, something jumped through the window and landed on his lap.

"Crazy mutt!" the sheriff yelled. "Get!" The dog licked his face as if it were basted with beef gravy. But the sheriff cut his meal short, and grabbed him by the ruff of the neck and put him outside. "I guess you came here to finish me off," the sheriff said. "Well, it didn't work, so good-bye."

The dog twirled in a circle. His propeller-like tail stirred the snow. His dance complete, he bounced on his hind legs and begged with his front paws. The sight was too much for Sheriff Durben to resist. He opened the door to let the dog get in, if he had a mind to, and he did.

"I have two rules, Agamemnon," the sheriff said. "Number one, keep your paws off the radio; number two, no pushing people off cliffs." The dog barked his agreement. The sheriff's stomach rumbled. "I better go inside and get me something to eat." The dog barked, and the sheriff added, "Get *us* something to eat." Sheriff Durben opened the door, and then looked back at Agamemnon. "I'll leave the window open in case you decide to leave or have to go find a tree."

The dog whined, curled into a ball on the seat, and closed his eyes.

# Chapter XXIX

M ary sat between her mother and Toby at a table in the middle of the hall. Mary had a plate of food, but was unable to eat. Something was wrong, but she didn't know what. People were whispering, looking at her, and then turning away. She looked at her mom, but her mom was fingering the top of the table as if it had piano keys. Mary gave Toby a nudge, but he was on his second piece of pie and ignored her. Then, she really got nervous. Sheriff Durben entered the hall and gave her the eye.

Mary grabbed Toby by the hand, his pie eating hand.

"What do you want?" he asked.

"Don't you feel it?" she said. "Something's wrong."

Toby looked around the hall. People were talking and laughing, children were playing; the desert table still had plenty of pies and cakes.

"What are you talking about?" he asked. "It looks okay to me."

"It's not okay; even your dad's acting strange. He's been talking to those men in the corner ever since he got back. But he hasn't said a word to us."

"That's nothing," Toby replied. "He's been acting weird for two days." Toby paused. "Come to think of it so has Mom."

"Where is she?" Mary asked.

"She woke up with a belly ache this morning and decided to stay home."

Mary looked around and said, "I still think something is wrong."

"Maybe you're hungry," Toby said. "Why don't you get some chocolate cake? You like chocolate cake, don't you?"

"I can't eat," Mary answered. "My stomach feels funny, and my skin is tingling."

Toby gave her a funny look and went back to eating his pie Mary stayed on guard, fidgeting in her chair, waiting for something to happen. Finally, it did.

"Look at that," Mary said, pointing to the stage.

A man took a green tarpaulin off a large object positioned near the rear of the stage. The object had a familiar shape.

"That's the organ from the church," Mary said.

Toby looked and swallowed a bite of half-chewed pie. He lowered his head and said, "Now we're in for it."

The man folded the tarp into a square, pushed it aside with his foot, dusted himself off, and then picked up a crate that was concealed under the organ. As he placed it on the bench, Reverend Richmann jumped to his feet and rushed over to the crate, and in one quick motion pulled the lid off.

"Hallelujah!" Reverend Richmann shouted.

He held the statue in the air for all to see.

Pastor Amos stood and cried out, "Glory be to God!"

A host of people rushed the stage, all wanting to see the statue at the same time. Sheriff Durben went up and spoke to the man who had taken the tarp off the organ. After a brief conversation he went over and inspected the crate. Mary scooted down in her chair. Toby leaned forward on his arms and hid his face.

When the excitement lulled, Reverend Richmann returned the statue to the crate and clapped his hands to get everyone's attention.

"I think this would be a good time for the coral program to begin," he said. He turned to the people on the stage.

"Would you please return to your seats? We're going to need every inch of space."

Cynthia pushed herself away from the table, gave Mary a hug, and walked over to the organ. Suddenly, Mary felt abandoned and unprotected.

Sheriff Durben examined something in his hand. He seemed bewildered. His confusion continued as his eyes focused on Mary.

The sheriff walked to her table. His stride was slow and steady. His eyes had a piercing stare. Toby looked at the sheriff, then at Mary, and then moved his chair further away from the impending confrontation. Mary trembled as the sheriff approached, then froze when he stood behind her. She could hear him breathe--heavy at first, then calm.

"I think this belongs to you?" Sheriff Durben said in a shallow voice. He handed her a Silver Star. "I found it in a very curious place. You wouldn't know how it got there?" Mary started to speak, but the sheriff stopped her and said, "Come to think of it, some things are best left unsaid. I'm confused enough as it is, no sense making it worse." He smiled, patted her on the shoulder, winked at Toby, and walked away.

Mary leaned back and breathed easier. Toby gave her a hug, and then pretended it never happened.

The two choirs came forward, and, under the direction of the choir director from St. Andrew Church, formed one large choral group that filled the entire stage. Cynthia played the customary practice notes, after which, the choir director keyed the choir, raised her hand, and the program began.

The songs were joyous, the choir angelic. Mary felt at ease for the first time in days. Toby leaned over his plate and finished his pie. When the program came to the final song, a feather was seen in the center of the choir floating to the front of the stage. It adorned the hat of the diminutive lead singer.

A hush fell over the people. The organ played, and the lead singer sang, "Oh Holy Night." The first verse sung, the two choirs were one; their voices clear and pure. When the song was finished, silence took its place, and the choir members returned to their seats.

Anticipation followed. The children squirmed in their seats. It was time for Santa to appear. But when the front door creaked opened, Rosey entered with a woman clinging to his arm.

She was tall and trim with big brown eyes and long brown hair. As they walked into the hall they were greeted by a barrage of whispers wanting to know who she was, what was wrong with Rosey's face, and why was he wearing a blue, double-breasted suit instead of the red and white Santa costume. The children were equally bewildered when, all of a sudden, sleigh bells were heard.

"Ho! Ho! Ho!" Santa Honeycut cried out. He pushed aside the rear stage curtain, and made his grand entrance. Behind him wearing a suit of green was one of his helpers, dragging a heavy bag.

Honeycut stroked his cotton beard and fearfully studied the children who could hardly refrain from running forward. His eyes widened in anticipation of the inevitable. He looked at Rosey, ascended Santa's throne, and awaited the rush of boisterous bodies hurling themselves into his lap.

Rosey gave him a cheer, clapped his hands, and the stampede began.

A boy got a red fire truck, a girl a doll. Each child in order sat on Santa's lap and received a gift in return. The last gift dispensed, Santa, with a hearty "Ho, Ho, Ho" and a silent sigh of relief, made his escape.

Toby gave Mary a nudge as his father took center stage. Everyone's attention was on him except for the playful children, who occasionally bumped a toy car or truck against the table legs, or caused a doll to voice a prolonged "Mommy."

Jeffrey gazed out into the crowd, fixed his tie, and contentedly smiled as he nodded to Paul and the sheriff.

"Before we leave tonight," Jeffrey said, tugging his collar, "I have something to say. Usually the mayor is here to end the festivities with one of his long speeches, but he's been called out of town--another miracle." Jeffrey paused until the laughter faded. "Many of you are aware of what took place tonight. If not, you soon will be. We may never be able to fully explain what has happened, we can only give thanks." Jeffrey glanced at the statue. "I do, however, know that an innocent man was sent to prison."

Jeffrey motioned to Cynthia and smiled.

"Would you please come up here, Mrs. Klein?"

Cynthia couldn't move. Rosey walked over and escorted her to the stage. Whispers accompanied each step she took.

"Cynthia," Jeffrey said. "The courts are not always just or the verdicts always right. It's an imperfect system created by an imperfect society doing the best it can. Tonight we have an opportunity to correct a mistake and to ask your forgiveness. I talked to the Governor. He has agreed to release Sylvester into Sheriff Durben's custody and to have his case reopened. I will personally make sure that he is home before the week is out." Jeffrey took an envelope out of his pocket and handed it to Cynthia. "I said *home*, your home. That's the deed to the Cole house, small compensation for what your family's gone through." Jeffrey smiled. "It looks like we're going to be neighbors."

Rosey clapped, then Paul, and then, one by one, cheers filled the hall. Jeffrey took Cynthia by the hand and walked her back to her chair; explanations were passed from table to table.

Mary pinned the Silver Star on her dress and turned to her mother. "Do you think it was a miracle?"

THE END